THE DIVIDING

THE DIVIDING

JEFF GULVIN

Cover Design by Amy Gulvin

This edition first published in 2013 by:

Thistle Publishing
36 Great Smith Street
London
SW1P 3BU

ISBN13: 978-1-909869-06-6

DEDICATION

For my wife Kim and my daughters Amy and Chloe

Special thanks to David Haviland and Andrew Lownie

ONE

Before he left Texas John Q's mother told him that a person, their personality and everything, was pretty much fixed by the time they were seven years old. After that how they turned out was due to the things that happened to them and the people they met on the way. She said that life was not about the destination so much as the journey. His mother didn't talk like that very often and three days later he still couldn't figure what she meant.

He had come east to see his grandmother; was due to spend the summer painting her house and had never been this far from home on his own. He had never spent so much time on a bus either and he was thinking about that when it pulled over finally, a little way out of town. As he jumped down John Q spotted a car parked further down the road, a convertible with the roof back; next to it a woman and her teenage daughter were sitting on the grass while a black kid bent to the trunk.

Overhead the sun beat down like it could in Texas only in Texas the gulf wind never stopped blowing. With his bag hooked over one shoulder John Q considered the canteen of water he had refilled at the last service station. Hot as it was and stuck by the road like that, he figured those folks could do with a drink.

Dust roiled as the bus trundled past and the girl started to cough. She was still coughing when John Q got to the car.

'Kind of sticks in your throat doesn't it,' he said offering the canteen. 'Here, have some of this.'

Gratefully she took it from him.

'That's very kind,' her mother smiled at him, 'very thoughtful, thank you.'

John Q felt his cheeks glow slightly. 'You're welcome, ma'am.' He glanced to where the black kid was on one knee now where a tire was flat. 'You all need a hand there?' he asked.

The kid looked up. 'You ever change a tire?'

'I fixed plenty on a bicycle but I ain't fifteen yet, I never drove a car.'

'Ain't fifteen either,' the kid said. 'Can fix me a tire though, it ain't so different to a bicycle.'

Getting up he nodded to the canteen. 'Can I get me some of that?'

The girl passed the water across and he took a drink and wiped his mouth on the back of his hand. John Q looked at the tire then at the spare on the lid of the trunk and that seemed pretty flat too.

'Neither of them holding any air,' the kid stated. 'Know how to work a wheel jack, do you?'

Stripping off his jacket, John Q got down next to him and the kid showed him where to place the jack. 'Pump her some,' he said, 'only not before I loosen these lug nuts.'

John Q could feel the girl's gaze on him. She was around his age, maybe a little younger and she was pretty. When he glanced up at her she looked away.

The black kid worked the lug nuts loose then John Q pumped the handle on the jack. When the wheel lifted clear of the ground they waggled it off the hub. The black kid unscrewed the cap on the valve stem and pressed the little nipple to make sure all the air was out then laid the wheel on the ground. Selecting a set of irons from the tool kit, he began to prise off the tire.

He paused for a moment to wipe the sweat where it studded his brow. 'There's a tire pump in the trunk,' he said as he worked the inner tube loose. 'You-all fetch her and we'll see where this tube's wore out.'

John Q went to fetch the pump and the black kid told him there was a patch kit back there as well.

'It's very kind of you to help,' the woman said. 'Are you headed into town?'

'Yes, ma'am,' John Q told her. 'Been cooped up on that bus clear out from Texas and I couldn't wait to get off.'

'You-all found them patches?' the kid called.

John Q rummaged in the trunk pocket, located the tin containing the patches and glue and took it over to where the tube was laid out. Fitting the pump to the valve stem he pumped the tube till it was fat and they all heard the hissing sound. They bent to the tube the four of them and it was the girl who spotted the hole. She pressed a finger to it, crouching close enough to John Q that he could smell the way she was sweating slightly and he felt his heart start to thump and his mouth go dry and heat flush his cheeks as it had just a few minutes before.

The black kid scrabbled in the tin for some chalk, marked the spot where the girl had her finger and then she let go. They sat back while he worked the valve and the air ushered out. Taking a drink himself John Q passed the water canteen once more. 'What's your name?' he asked the girl.

'Willow, Willow Flood.'

'And yours?' her mother said.

'John Quarrie, ma'am; but folks call me John Q. I'm out of San Saba County, Texas; come here to visit with my grandma.'

The black kid had selected a patch and was prising the top off the tube of glue. He told John Q to use the lid of the kit where the edge was serrated to roughen up the rubber and when he had done that the kid pasted a little glue.

With the patch secure finally they pressed the inner tube back and then John Q took the irons and levered the tire onto the rim before they pumped it up once more.

'There you go,' the kid said. 'I guess you done fixed your first tire.'

John Q grinned. 'Make a mechanic of me yet. What's your name by the way, I'm John Q.'

'Pious,' the kid said. 'My name is Pious Noon.'

Between them they rolled the wheel back to the car and fitted it on the hub. 'You said how you were here to see your grandma,' Pious said. 'Staying with her long then are you?'

'The summer I guess. Quit school back in San Saba County already and my Uncle Frank put a word in with a rancher he knows so I got a job to go to in the fall. Mr Whitfield his name is,' John Q was glancing at Willow as he spoke. 'Got a spread that's part of what used to be the XIT Ranch up in the Texas panhandle. You ever hear of that place, did you?'

Pious shook his head.

'Some parcel of land I reckon. They say it was so big it covered ten counties though it's broke up now, of course. My uncle Frank worked there for a couple of years before he volunteered to go settle a town they said was lawless on account of the oil.'

'Settle, what d'you mean settle?'

John Q shrugged. 'Give it some law I suppose.'

'So he's a cop your uncle, is he?'

'Nope, he's retired. But he was a cop. Texas Ranger, you ever hear of them?'

'Course I heard of them, sure.'

They were finished with the car, the wheel back on and the jack lowered, it was ready to go. Again Mrs Flood thanked them. 'I can't give you boys a ride,' she said, 'because we're headed out of town right now and we don't have room. But when you get to the square go over to see Mrs Austin at the ice cream parlor and get yourselves a couple of sundaes. Tell her I'll be by to pay her on my way home.'

'Thank you, ma'am,' John Q said, 'that's real nice of you but I got to cut along.'

'Yeah, actually I got to get going too.' Pious looked like he might fancy a sundae but felt he ought to decline.

'All right then,' Mrs Flood said. 'I tell you what: Pious, we have ice cream up at the Bluff. I'll make sure your mama takes some when she leaves out and you can have it when she gets home.'

John Q watched Willow as she climbed into the passenger seat. She smiled at him and he felt a little heat behind his ears and again his mouth was dry.

'Maybe I'll see you around,' he said.

She did not reply. She just nodded and then her mother eased the car back onto the road.

For a long moment the two boys stood there watching as it headed towards the forest. John Q glanced at his hands where they were covered in dirt. Not just his hands but his jeans and the sleeves of his shirt.

'How far to town, Pious?' he said.

'Half mile maybe I suppose.'

'All right then, let's get going.'

As they walked John Q was the one doing the talking. 'My daddy was born in Spanish Fork,' he said. 'Left out when his daddy, my granddaddy, never come back from the First World War.'

Pious nodded where he ambled alongside.

'Took a hunk of shrapnel in the chest and all grandma got from the army was a telegram telling her he wasn't coming back.'

Again Pious nodded.

'My daddy,' John Q went on, 'he took off a few years after, headed over to San Saba County where I live at and married my mother. Took a job working for the paper and been doing it ever since.' He looked sideways. 'Only twice in my life have I visited. First time was around Christmas about five years back. The Japs were flying airplanes into our ships and it was all anybody talked about.'

'Stopped making cars,' Pious said.

'What?'

'Cadillac, Chevrolet, Ford. Up at the big house where my mama works they got an M-24 Mr Barra likes to ride in and they stopped making that when the war started and only just now got the last of them out.'

Eyebrows arched, John Q squinted at him. 'How come you know stuff like that?'

Pious shrugged. 'Like cars is all I suppose.'

———

TWO

Willow was thinking about that boy and the way he kept glancing at her all the time he and Pious were fixing the wheel. She thought about the canteen of water and how their fingers had touched when he passed it across. She thought about those blue jeans he was wearing and how nobody around here wore those. She thought about what he had said to Pious about ranching and wondered what it would be like to work all day on a horse.

They were back on the road now, heading for Bluff Bridge and she hadn't really wanted to go. She hadn't said anything because today was the anniversary of her grandmother's death and the first time her mother had to go to the bridge without her dad. That meant Willow had to be there because if she didn't her mother would be on her own. She decided it wasn't so bad now they were almost there, and if she hadn't come along she would never have seen that boy.

A few miles further they were deep in the woods, the road like a switchback and she could hear a noise in the distance like a rush of wind only it wasn't wind it was water. They came to the bridge finally, and her mother pulled into the turnout.

For a moment they sat there then her mother switched off the engine and Willow could really hear the water now.

'It's so loud,' she said. 'Momma, is it always so loud?'

Eyes tight, her mother nodded. Between the seats she had some flowers wrapped in waxed paper that Mama Sox had cut fresh from the garden that morning.

'It's loud because it's deep,' she said. 'The way that ground is under the bridge, the way that gorge is sort of shaped like a funnel, it echoes, Willow; it accentuates the sound.'

Together they walked to the middle of the bridge where Willow peered over the wall. A hundred feet down the land sloped into the cone shaped pit her mother had just described. The trees were sparse; their trunks narrow, growing almost horizontally in places with their branches sticking straight up in the air. She could see the rocks where they were black and gray; she could see where they were sharp and smooth and how the water seemed to boil round the wreckage below.

The Pit, a massive whirlpool where a fork of the river caught in a hole worked so deep in the bedrock that people said it ran all the way to the gates of Hell. Her mother told her how it was like some gigantic plug-hole that sucked at whatever fell in and never let it out again. It was where Willow's grandmother had drowned twenty-five years before.

Drunk on moonshine she stumbled across the road outside Koontz Cafe. A Model T Ford parked out front with the key still in the dash, it was driven by Morgan J. They had come into town together but Laurel was a squatter from the island and squatters from the island liked to drink. While Morgan J sat down to some dinner she went off to see what she could find.

Corn mash whiskey, she came back blind with it; laughing and giggling she stumbled across that highway with one shoe on and the other in her hand. From the window of the cafe Morgan J saw her as she stumbled round the front of the car. Somehow she cranked the handle and the car shuddered into life. She was so drunk she almost fell over but she grabbed the fender then got in where the driver sat. As she did that a sheriff's car came around the corner, the young deputy spotted her and slowed right down. At the same time Morgan J leapt up from his table and came rushing outside. But already Laurel was spinning the car around and he only just managed to jump in.

Opening the throttle she took off down the highway heading for the landing and the boat that would take her home. Morgan J tried to grab the wheel, tried to make her slow down; desperately he tried to get her to stop. But she lashed out with a fist and it was all he could do to hold on as she weaved right across the road.

Willow knew the story by heart but this was the first time she had actually read the article they had written in the newspaper. Her mother had kept it all these years to remind her how things had been reported. She read it every year without fail wondering if she would ever see justice. What had not been reported, what she remembered and nobody else seemed to, was the fact that Morgan J had been around all summer and it was him that liked to get drunk and not her mother at all.

————

Together Pious and John Q walked into Spanish Fork. It had been so long since John Q had been there he could barely remember the town. The central square was dominated by a gothic looking building set back on a grassy knoll. Pious said it was where the town council met and where the sheriff's office was. With pillars out front it overlooked a statue of Light-Horse Harry Lee. Pious said Harry was Robert E Lee's daddy and from Virginia not Georgia at all.

'So what's his statue doing here?' John Q asked.

Pious just shrugged his shoulders. 'Don't know really. It's Light Horse County I guess.'

It was no kind of answer but it was all John Q was going to get and it didn't matter anyway. It was too hot to be thinking about stuff like that. Above them the sky was clear and blue and the sun frazzled freshly laid road tar into patches of treacle-like mush. Taking John Q's empty water canteen to the fountain set aside for blacks, Pious re-filled it for him. Across the other side of the square a bunch of older men were sitting under the canopy on the sidewalk outside the lunch room door. Further down the street a shoe-shine boy hovered with his box of brushes and beyond him a rag picker pushed his trolley-cart full of old clothes.

Smoking cigarettes and drinking coffee, the old men watched the two boys across the way.

'Last time I was here I was ten years old,' John Q said where he sat on the grass.

Pious was glancing furtively at the group of men. 'I reckon I best take off.'

'Why, what's up?'

'Thanks for helping out with that tire just now but I'd best be on my way.'

John Q watched him cross the square and walk the dust blown street all the way to the where the railroad tracks carried the height of a cinder rise.

Crossing the square himself now, the sun beat against his scalp and he wished he had brought his hat. The heat was moist, the air humid; he walked up the sidewalk to where the old men were gathered under the shade of the canopy.

'Howdy,' he said. 'I was wondering if maybe you could help me. I'm looking to find Mrs Quarrie. I don't know if you-all know her, she lives on Riverview Road.'

One old guy with a shrivelled face and crumpled hat squinted at him as he scraped a cigarette from a pack. 'You're talking about Grandma Q?'

'Yes sir. She's my grandma on my daddy's side.'

'And you don't know where she lives?'

'No sir, not exactly: I was only ten when I came here the last time and that was with my family.'

'So how'd you get here this time?'

'Just now sir? On the bus.'

'From where at?'

'San Saba County, Texas.'

The old man gestured across the road to the fountain where Pious had filled the canteen.

'Well son,' he said, 'you're in Georgia now and that's a long ways from Texas or maybe you ain't never been told.'

His grandmother was sitting in a rocking chair on her porch when he walked up to the house. He couldn't figure what that first guy had been talking about but another of the men had given him directions to Riverview Road. He made his way across town, passing the bank and the indoor food market and the pool hall where one of the lights was blinking on and off. From there it was another few blocks before the town gave out and it wasn't long before he could hear gulls crying which suggested he was getting close.

Riverview was a dirt road that followed the course of the river as it cut through the gorge. Five years since he had been here, Christmas in 1941, he remembered all the talk had been about Pearl Harbor and what it was going to mean. For some reason it made him think about his dad's old Terraplane, the sedan model, though his mother had favored the coupe. That was the longest road trip he and his sister had ever taken, all the way across country they had gotten here finally and there was Grandma Q setting that rocker just like she was now only then it had been cold enough to snow.

Standing at the gate he felt awkward suddenly, not knowing quite what to do and realizing he had never been alone with her before. She didn't really know him. He didn't know her and he thought she looked older than she ought to somehow. He could smell the cherry flavored tobacco she smoked in an old style clay pipe that his dad said was no good for her but she liked to take a match to anyway. His dad said how it had been his father's pipe and she only took it up after he never came home from the war.

On a small table next to her John Q could see a coffee cup and half-eaten slice of bread dripping in molasses. He remembered the blue and white striped can from before. His grandma had a sweet tooth all right, but now she had the pipe clamped between her lips and her eyes closed under the brim of her hat.

On the walk out here John Q had stopped to pluck a few stems of wild columbine because before he left home, his mother reminded him that his grandmother did not have many visitors and that there wasn't a woman alive who did not like to get flowers. He had a bunch of them in his hand, still hovering at the gate which had been white once though it was flaking badly now. It was one of the jobs he had promised his father he would get to while he was here.

Still his grandma rocked, still her eyes remained closed under that hat and all the while tight little puffs of smoke were escaping her narrow lips.

'Grandma,' he called finally. 'It's young John out here come from Texas. I brought you some flowers.'

She sat a moment longer then opened her eyes and peeked from under the hat. 'Well don't just stand there,' she said, 'come on in.'

Pushing open the gate he walked up the path with his bag in one hand and the canteen over his shoulder and presented her with the wild flowers. Pipe still in her mouth she took them from him with a smile. 'You've grown tall, boy,' she said, 'must be taller than your daddy now.'

Inside, the old place smelled musty; of lavender maybe, what he thought was an old person's smell. But it was nice and cool at least and his grandma told him that at this time of year she kept the curtains pulled and the windows closed while the sun was out to keep the heat from the house.

She showed him down the hallway to a room at the back he had shared with his sister the last time they had been here. It was all coming back to him, how his folks had had his grandma's bedroom while she slept on a put-you-up in the lounge. He remembered she had told them that she didn't need privacy because she was last to turn in at night and first up in the morning and by the time anybody else was up she was already making breakfast.

To the side of the house was an old lean-to built over an ancient car: beyond it his grandfather's workshop and out back the yard where his grandmother liked to spend her time. At the far end of the yard a flight of rickety wooden steps led down to the river.

He remembered that the current wasn't too strong just there and how the bank recessed into an oval shaped pool and he recalled his father telling him it was where the old woman used to bathe in the days before she had an indoor tub.

———

THREE

When he got up on Saturday morning his grandma was in the kitchen cooking pancakes on the timber fed stove. Back home his mother had one powered by propane like everybody else, but his grandma still used stove-wood. She still had the old style ice box as well; no electric, just the cabinet and the blocks of ice the delivery boy brought out from the grocery store. Last year his father had tried to buy her a new Frigidaire from the Sears catalogue but she said she was happy with what she knew.

John Q sat down at the table where she served him a plate of pancakes smothered in the black molasses and a glass of milk. After breakfast he went over to his grandpa's workshop and found a pair of paint scrapers and package of unopened glass paper that worked both wet and dry. Starting out front he began to rub down the paintwork on the fence, working each panel thoroughly with the scraper first and when all the big flakes were off he used the paper to make it smooth.

He worked all morning sanding the whole of the front section and when he was done his grandma took a long look at it. With a nod she told him he had done a good job and gave him two dollars to go into town and buy paint.

John Q gestured to the fence on the other side of the gate. 'Grandma,' he said, 'don't you want me to get to that section before I start in with the paint?'

'Well, son, if you want to that's up to you. But this here section's all prepared nice and smooth and I'd kind of like to see how she's going to look. The Mercantile on Maple,' she suggested. 'That's where the paint's at. You can't miss the place, they always got coffee going and it's where the trucks are parked out front.'

The sun was at its height now and John Q felt the heat beginning to burn his scalp.

'Grandma,' he said. 'I'm fourteen years old, will be fifteen here in a little bit and back home in Texas I wear a hat on account of I'm horseback a lot of the time. I clean forgot to bring it with me and I don't know why. But that sun sure is hot, do you got one I could borrow maybe?

The screen door flapped as she went inside. John Q sat on the stoop and thought about how it was hotter than it had been yesterday and sweat seemed to boil the stalks of his hair. Moments later his grandma was back and she carried a short brimmed Stetson that looked like it was fresh out of the box.

'It was your grandpa's,' she told him, 'seven and three eighths, hardly got to wear it before he took off for the war.'

John Q put it on and it fitted pretty well. His grandma stood before him pulling lightly at the brim. 'Wear it a little on one side like he did,' she suggested. 'You know how much you look like him? Did I show you his picture yet?'

'No ma'am, you didn't.'

'I guess I'll look it out later. He would've liked that you're wearing it and you're old enough I guess. What is it you-all said you're going to be here in a little bit?'

'Fifteen, in a couple of weeks.'

'Well that's a man right there. You quit school already, didn't you?'

'Yes ma'am I did.'

'So what is it you're going to be working at, when you get home to Texas I mean?'

'I figured I'd do ranch work for a while maybe, but I always wanted to be a cop; figured I'd give it a couple of years then try for the Texas Rangers.'

'Like your Uncle Frank?'

'Yes ma'am,' he looked quizzical. 'I didn't know you knew about him.'

'Son,' she said, laying a hand on his shoulder. 'There ain't a person in this country hasn't heard of your Uncle Frank. I remember how he settled the town of Navasota, Texas when he wasn't twenty-four years old. Later on of course it was him dealt with Bonnie and Clyde.' She muttered then softly to herself. 'That pair, I swear they've been trying to immortalize them ever since.'

'Trying to do what now?' John Q asked her.

'Immortalize: remember folk not as they were but as other folk would've wanted them to be. Make a hero out of people when in reality they ain't no good. Kind of thing happens all the time.'

John Q walked into town carrying the money she had given him to spend on paint and some Stoddard Solvent to clean the brushes when he was done. He was thinking about what his grandma had said about Clyde Barrow and Bonnie Parker and how that was something his uncle never talked about but everybody else did, of course. He supposed it was a fact that Frank Hamer was about the most famous Texas Ranger there had ever been but he was modest and never really talked about what he did. He had told John Q how when this last war broke out in Europe however, he wrote the King of England offering his services as a bodyguard in case the Germans rolled in with their tanks. John Q called him Uncle Frank on account of his mother said it was polite, but he was actually his godfather and a cousin to the family on his mother's side.

Making the corner at Palisades and Maple Street he came to the Chevy dealer he had passed yesterday. They had a brand new Fleetmaster in the showroom that was advertised at last year's price of "just twelve hundred and eighty dollars". John Q pressed his face to the window steaming up the glass and thinking how much money that was this year, never mind last. Black paint and bull-nosed with polished fenders and white-wall tires, there were three horizontal strips to the grille. Back in Texas, Tyler Franklin's dad had spent the money he made selling seventy-five dollar war bonds to buy one of these, he used to cruise Main Street in it all the time.

In the square he took a drink from the fountain set aside for white people then crossed the street and wandered past the ice cream parlor. At the drugstore he paused on the wooden sidewalk as a car came around the corner; the convertible from yesterday, Willow and her mother they pulled up right where he stood.

Thumbing his hat back from his forehead John Q felt his mouth go dry. Willow saw him and looked as if she was going to smile but a little color touched her cheeks and she turned away.

'John Q,' her mother said. 'How are you today?'

'Just fine, Mrs Flood, ma'am; thank you.'

'Did you make it to your grandmother's okay? I know Mrs Quarrie, though it's a while since I've said hello.'

John Q was looking at Willow. 'Yes, ma'am,' his voice was a little thick in his throat. 'I made it just fine and I'm sure she'd like to see you. I don't think she has many visitors.'

'Then I'll be sure to come and visit with her.' Mrs Flood nodded to the drugstore. 'We're going inside for a soda. Can I fetch one for you?'

'Yes, ma'am, thank you. Dr Pepper would be just fine.' Still he was looking at Willow but she seemed to be deliberately avoiding his eye.

'Do you want to come inside,' Mrs Flood asked, 'sit down at the counter where it's nice and cool?'

'No, ma'am, thank you. I got to get to the Mercantile.'

They disappeared into the darkened interior and John Q heard movement behind him and looked round to see Pious standing at the corner.

'See the car done made it then,' Pious said, 'Miss Willow and her mom. Reckon you and me could go into business.'

'How you doing, Pious,' John Q said.

Pious nodded to the car. 'They drive in most every Saturday. Before he got killed in the war it used to be her daddy that brought Miss Willow. That family is from Savannah, Georgia I guess, but they live up at Spanish Bluff now.' He flapped a hand in an easterly direction. 'That's the big house I'm talking about, Mr Barra's place where my mama is the housekeeper. Old Mr Barra he adopted Mrs Flood when she was a bitty kid. Anyways, might-could be I'll be living there myself pretty soon, we're waiting on finding out.'

John Q nodded. 'Where'd you live at now?'

Pious gestured towards the railroad. 'South-city, other side of that cinder rise.'

Mrs Flood and Willow came out of the drugstore with a couple of bottles of Dr Pepper and two Popsicles. Mrs Flood passed a bottle of soda to John Q and the other to Pious then she broke a Popsicle and offered them each a side. 'I saw you through the window, Pious,' she said, 'thought you'd like something too.'

Willow stood there sucking soda through a straw in her white blouse and britches though she avoided John Q's eye.

'Pious,' Mrs Flood went on. 'Did your mother say anything to you about moving up to the Bluff?'

'Yes, ma'am she did.'

'Well it's not been decided completely yet and I suppose it'll depend on how Mr Barra is with his health and everything, but personally I think it's what we should do now that your brothers are off sharecropping.'

Back at his grandma's house that afternoon, John Q took a paint brush to the picket fence and all the time he was working he could not stop thinking about that girl. The way she had only sort of glanced at him this morning, not really seeming to notice him and not saying anything at all. Yesterday she had been a bit more chatty and that didn't make much sense. But then again, back in Texas Billy Culpepper told him that's what girls did when they liked you so maybe that was it. Billy reckoned that when girls sort of ignored you, acted as if you weren't there, it didn't mean what you thought it did. John Q wasn't sure; the trouble with Billy was he figured he was some kind of expert when it came to girls; always talking about them, always looking at them; always combing his hair.

John Q hadn't had a girlfriend since Betty Moore a year back in high school. Her family moved away after Christmas, and since then he had been too busy helping Billy's dad with his cutting horses to go out with anybody new.

He went to sleep thinking about Willow and he woke up thinking about her as well. It was still dark outside and with the window wide open the cool of the pre-dawn drifted up from the river. His boots seemed to have found their way under the bed and he hunted them down and hauled them on then went through to the kitchen where his grandma was making scrambled eggs.

'Morning, Johnny,' she said. 'That fence's looking pretty good after that first lick of paint.'

'Yes, ma'am; figured I'd get another on her this morning lessen you want me to start with the scraper on the other side.'

'I guess the scraper would be a good idea,' she said. 'Only not today, today's Sunday and though I ain't a one for church or anything like that your grandpa used to keep the Sabbath Day.' With a smile she looked over her shoulder. 'Today's all yours, son; there is no work on Sunday.'

Taking a cloth to the handle John Q lifted the coffee pot where it warmed on the stove. 'You mean that, Grandma?' he said.

'Sure I mean it. Wouldn't say her if I didn't. Take the boat if you have a mind. Only be careful if you try to cross the shoals: those tides reverse where they hit the sandbanks and it takes a keen eye to get her through. Further up the channel you got that hole in the sea bed we call Bull Shark Bay and that's no place to be messing with, trust me.'

John Q sipped milky coffee. 'Grandma,' he said, 'there ain't much about a horse I can't figure on account of all the work I done with Billy Culpepper's dad, but I ain't no use in a boat. Reckon I need somebody along that knows the water.' He paused for a moment then he added: 'I was going to ask you if you knew which house Pious Noon lived at.'

Spooning eggs onto a plate his grandmother took a moment to think. 'You talking about Mama Sox's youngest boy, you figure it's him you want to be hanging around with? I know his momma well enough and she's a sweet lady but this is Georgia and there ain't many white kids go hanging around with blacks.'

'Ain't hanging around with him so much, Grandma; I just saw him when I got here is all. Helped him fix a tire on Mrs Flood's car and right now he's the only kid in town I know.'

His grandmother dished eggs onto the plate and handed it to him. 'There's bacon warming and biscuits,' she indicated the oven. 'I got no truck with who you make friends with, Johnny. I'm just saying that around here folks have their own way.' She sighed then and gazed into space. 'Mrs Flood was it, you said you were helping?'

'Yes ma'am, she had a flat tire on her car.'

'It's a long time since I saw her and it's a long time since I saw Mama Sox.' She smiled then at some memory. 'You know, I can't recollect what her given name is but everybody calls her Mama Sox on account of she wears white cotton socks no matter what dress she's wearing and no matter what kind of shoes or what day. This morning for example,' she threw out a hand, 'she'll be in church wearing a pair of white cotton socks with her best heels, never seen her any other way.'

Sitting down at the table she poured herself some coffee. 'Back when she was a kid Mama lived over on Half-Mile Island and she never wore shoes leave alone socks. People lived in the old slave quarter, huts they fixed up that belonged to the McElroy's back in the day. Only place in the state of Georgia where white and black people lived together, only trouble was nobody on the mainland would talk to them, not white to white or black to black, not when they came over here. Me, I was a midwife in those days, my job to register the births. I had my boat and I'd go over there and deliver babies because if I didn't mother or child or both would likely die. Cassie Flood herself was born over there though you wouldn't think it to see her today.'

Sitting back in the chair she stared out the window where the first rays of sunlight were breaking through. 'Mama Sox helped me out with that birth and she wasn't but ten years old. The century itself was only ten years old I reckon and that was the last time I was called over there and Cassie the last time I registered a birth.' She made an open-handed gesture.

'Those cribs, huts or whatever you want to call them; those islanders fixed them up pretty good. There weren't just whites and blacks, but Indians, Guale some of them; could trace their line back to before the Yamasee had their amalgamation.' Getting to her feet now she swept a hand through her hair. 'One of these days I'll tell you about that but not right now so go ahead and eat your eggs.'

Walking into town John Q got to the square just as the gas station was opening up. His grandmother told him that Mr Johnson was a God-fearing man and he only opened Sundays until midday.

He had two pumps out front and John Q set down the metal jerry-can his grandma had found for him in the back of her Ford. She told him the fuel tank on her skiff's motor was almost certainly empty and if he wanted to get it running he would need some gas. Mr Johnson's son came out and pumped a gallon and John Q watched the glass bubble at the top of the pump empty and refill again. He still had two-bits left over from the paint and spirit he had bought yesterday and he went inside to pay. Not wanting to haul the jerry-can all over town he asked Mr Johnson if he could pick it up on his way home.

Leaving the square, he headed for the railroad where it was raised on the cinder causeway. Climbing the tightly packed stones he was atop the line where he had a vantage point that gave him a view across town. South was the black-quarter where the cabins were tumbledown and beaten up, cobbled together with bits of plywood and tarpaulin; layers of roofing tin. They reminded him of how most Mexicans lived back in Texas.

The cabins ran right up to the cinder ridge and he figured that when a train came through the nearest homes would shake so badly they would about fall down. A little further down the north side he picked out a couple of abandoned railroad cars, two lying on their sides and one upright that looked a little less busted up than the others. It had gold lettering on the side. On the lot out front he spied a couple of wrecked automobiles and between them a few coals were glowing in a makeshift pit. As he watched a scruffy looking man stepped down from the railroad car with a coffee pot he settled over the fire.

He found Pious' place a few streets away from the tracks. One of the better kept homes it had glass in the windows and a proper fitting door. He knocked on it. Dark inside, no electric and no hurricane lamp; it smelled a little dank maybe but he could see clean clothes drying on the line.

'Who is it?' Pious' voice lifted from the other side of the door.

'John Q, you coming out or shall I come in?'

The door opened and Pious came out stuffing his shirt into his pants. 'What-all you doing back here?' he said. 'White folks don't come south of the railroad, not unless they's cops.'

'Yeah well you're the only kid in town I know right now and I got a question I want to ask you.'

'Yeah, what's that?'

'You know how to run a boat?'

'Sure I know how to run a boat. That's the Spanish River we're living on or maybe you hadn't noticed.'

Head to one side John Q rolled his eyes. 'Well anyway, my grandma's got a skiff with an outboard on her and I just now bought some gas. I ain't any kind of sailor and I can't run a boat by myself on account of those tides you got going and all the sharks in the bay. But I got the day off house painting, Pious and I got a hankering to explore Half-Mile-Island. What say, bud; you and me go cross the divide?'

———

FOUR

Up at the Barra house, Willow ate a bowl of bran and grape nuts smothered in ice cold milk. Sitting at the kitchen table she could hear the squeak of rubber on wood and through the French windows she saw her great-grandpa leaning on his sticks. He had a cancer that her mother said would kill him and she had to prepare for it now. He was still getting around though, and with his hands buckled over the head of each cane, he studied his property.

The lawn needed mowing; it was the first thing he had commented on when they got back from the hospital the other day and he had summoned Albert from where he was trimming live oaks that bordered the drive. Calmly, Albert told him he would get to the lawn in a couple of days. He said that spring had been overly hot this year and with summer looking as if it was going to burn up he thought the grass ought to be allowed to grow some before it was cut.

Finishing the cereal, Willow took her bowl and spoon to the sink where Mama Sox was elbow deep in suds. 'You sure you had enough?' the housekeeper asked her.

'Yes, ma'am, thank you.'

'All right then. You-all be careful out there by the pool if its swimming you're at. That there sun's awful hot even for Spanish Bluff.'

'Mama,' Willow said. 'Is it true you might be coming to live up here, bringing Pious and Eunice with you?'

'Yes'm, in that apartment above the garage.' Mama nodded through the window now. 'Since Mr Barra done away with having a chauffeur that place been empty and it's got its own bathtub and toilet and all.'

Willow leaned on the drainer beside her. 'Momma told me that Eunice was too young to stay home all summer on her own. I haven't seen her in a long time. How old is she now?'

'She'll be eight on the 10th of July.'

Her mother was outside by the pool and Willow thought she looked troubled. Something in her eyes, it wasn't only because her grandpa was so sick and that they had just had the anniversary of her mother's death, it was the news that Morgan Junior was coming home.

Her great-grandpa's only son, Morgan J bothered her mother more than anybody Willow knew. He bothered her too come to that, and with her father not coming back from the war there was no longer anyone to step in his way. It was a fact that Morgan J had never accepted the idea that his father had adopted Willow's mother in the first place.

'Momma,' she said as she crossed the patio. 'Is it all right if I take the boat?'

Her mother looked up. Then she turned her cheek to a wind that wasn't there. The day was still and sunburnt and that meant the sea would be too.

'I guess,' she said, 'but take care when you cross the shoals. And don't be all day, Willow. Morgan J is supposed to be showing up tonight and I want you back before he gets here, okay?'

————

'It ain't the divide it's called The Dividing,' Pious said as they climbed the cinder rise, 'that spot where the tides run back.' He glanced towards the camp fire where the man John Q had seen earlier was sitting in a seat he must've ripped out of one of the automobiles.

'Noble Landry,' Pious told him, 'just got out of the county workhouse after six months laying sewer pipe. You see those guys wearing their striped pajamas, work detail up on the highway. I figure Noble's been in the work house more than he's been out of it and his brother a sheriff's deputy. Chase Landry, he likes to put the hurt on black boys he thinks might be trying to hook up with white girls and he's real mean about it too.' He sniffed then and his eyes were cold. 'He and Skipwith used to go after my daddy all the time.'

John Q looked sideways at him. 'Where's he at your daddy, share-cropping with your brothers, is he now?'

Sliding down the north side of the railroad tracks Pious shook his head. 'No sir, he ain't sharecropping, he's in the cemetery is where he's at. Got hisself blind drunk one Thursday on some kind of corn mash some-body colored to make it look like bourbon whiskey.' He gestured across town. 'Pitched off the sidewalk in front of a truck about squashed him flatter than a stepped on snake.'

'I'm sorry.' John Q was shocked.

'Well don't be because I ain't, was meaner than a junkyard dog; never brought home no money and liked to beat up on Mama all the time.'

Collecting the gas from Mr Johnson they headed back to Riverview Road where they found John Q's grandmother in her print dress and straw hat, barefoot and cutting back lupines with a pair of pruning shears.

'Pious,' she said, 'that skiff of mine's got a new engine.'

'It does?'

'Yes it does, bought it from Mr Livermore over in Rutherford, six-year old Evinrude and she's temperamental.'

'On account of how she's got a magneto I guess you mean.' Pious nod-ded like an expert now. 'Spark that ain't hooked up to the fuel or anything: it's just a separate operation is all and that's what folks can't get their heads around.' He smiled then showing white teeth. 'It don't matter, Mrs Q: I know how to get her working.'

'I figured you might.' The old woman smiled. 'Your daddy was more accomplished around an engine than anybody I ever knew: didn't matter if it was an automobile, boat or motorcycle. I guess he taught you pretty good.'

'No ma'am, matter of fact he didn't teach me at all.' Pious' expression was grim. 'I saw what he did all right and done taught myself. Figured I might make something of it, they say Preacher Anderson's going to open a shop in south-city on account of some black folk getting vehicles.'

'Well, if he does he should look no further for his mechanic.' The old lady considered her grandson then. 'You got gas I guess, so you're good to go. Take something to eat with you, there's cheese in the ice box and baloney you can slice and dill pickles. You can fix a sandwich apiece and there's plenty fresh water over there on the island.'

Down at the jetty they filled the gas tank that was fitted on top of the motor. The boat was narrow and made of wood, little more than a pirogue really with two bench seats and the outboard fixed in the stern. Pious set the magneto to run and the switch to prime then wrapped the rope coil around the starter and hauled on it. The engine caught first time and sitting down with a satisfied smile on his face he adjusted the primer again.

———

Further downriver Willow was guiding her own boat. A skiff her mother had picked out a few years back, small and sturdy with a Johnson Seahorse motor they claimed was just about indestructible.

She followed the bends in the river heading for Half-Mile Island where salt marsh covered the western shore and woodland scattered the highlands all the way to Fermanagh where the broken stones were all that remained of the McHenry mansion. In some places the trees grew right down to the water; tangled folds of live oak and yellow pine split by mud banks and sandbars, fresh water creeks that criss-crossed from shore to shore.

The island had been her playground for as long as Willow could remember. It had been her mother's backyard. For the first ten years of her life, she had lived there and that's what galled Morgan J. Back then the only folk over there were squatters, what people called vagrants; those who lived on what her mother said were the margins of society.

Willow didn't know what had made her great-grandpa adopt her like he had; all she knew was that her mother had been orphaned before she was eleven and had gone from one Baptist Mission Cottage to another.

No matter where the state put her, she would run off and make her way back to Half-Mile-Island and maybe the old man had just admired her pluck because one day he showed up at the orphanage where she had been placed in Rutherford. A few months after that she was living at Spanish Bluff and a year later her last name was changed to Barra from Brown.

As Willow grew up her mother showed her how to pilot a boat and together they explored every inch of the island. She taught her all about the McElroys who had owned the plantations in the north and the McHenry's who worked the south. She taught her about the great fire that destroyed the house at Fermanagh back in 1850 and how, after the McHenrys left, they sold their land to the McElroys.

Long after the plantations were done with, Jane McElroy married Morgan Barra of Savannah who turned a blind eye to the squatters who had taken over the slave cabins. Willow knew how her mother had come into the world without a father and back then that was even more looked down on than it was now. She had heard the story both from her mother and Mama Sox though they both said that none of the islanders were bothered by it. Probably they were too busy with their own worries because all the time they were living there Morgan J was threatening to kick them out of their homes. Ever since anybody could remember he had wanted to build a playground for rich people and whenever he crossed the water he would tell the squatters they had to go. Eventually they got so weary of it they did start to drift away and her mother said that by 1930 the entire settlement was deserted yet nothing had been built to this day.

Willow was beyond the shoals now and with the hull no longer being slapped and buffeted by reversing tides she guided the skiff to the where the Orange Blossom River spilled into the bay. The sun was high and the sky clear and as she closed the throttle a heron lifted from where it nested in the salt marsh.

This was her place; her sanctuary, there wasn't a patch of grass she had not discovered and she knew every inch of dirt from the settlement to the cotton groves and the sugar cane trail that ran to where the McElroy house still stood up there on the hill.

Tying up at the mooring, she gazed across the marshlands and thought that if there was any way they could keep Morgan J out of it, she would fix up that house and live there when she grew up.

Walking the beach the wind blew across her skin. Picking a trail through the marsh she kept one eye peeled for water moccasins. There weren't many creatures that bothered her, not even alligators so long as they kept out of her way, but those cotton-mouth snakes made her skin creep like she didn't know what. They way they would glide through the muddy water in the ditches; the way they would slither up trees and curl around a branch with their heads swinging back and forth. If they bit you your flesh would rot and that thought was so awful it sent a shiver the length of her spine.

Leaving the marsh she climbed the hill to open country and paused to watch a band of wild horses. She had no idea how many roamed here but there were probably hundreds and they were wild all right and some of them were beautiful in a rough and ready sort of way. Her mother said they had been left over from when the Spanish occupied the island a couple of hundred years before.

Willow walked north. She skirted mud flats and marshland; creeks that trailed to the sea. She passed Cooper's Bluff and the great willow she had been named after then heading inland she walked the Sugar Cane Trail to the pond at Yellow Pine. Half an hour later she stepped from the trees onto the low escarpment where the old trail dipped to the cluster of cabins still standing on the terraces where her mother had been born.

Beyond them the lagoon lay walled by sunken rocks with the only passage falling between a pair of mitre shaped stones everyone referred to as The Shark's Teeth. The trail down to it was deep and wide where it had been shaped by footsore slaves and the wheels of corn-ricks and cane planters. Willow liked to swim in that lagoon because the water was warm and clear and blue. It was rare for a shark to get in and when one did mostly all it wanted to do was get out again. Unless of course it was a bull shark; then it would hunt swimmers as bull sharks seemed wont to do.

There was no shark in there today though, with the water as clear as it was she would be able to pick out its shadow. She didn't see any shadow. What she saw was a boat piloted by Pious Noon and that other boy sitting in the prow. For a long moment she stared at them. With Morgan J coming home she had things on her mind and she'd come over here because she had wanted to be on her own.

———

FIVE

By midday the heat was so intense there was nobody on the street, nobody save Noble Landry that is, making his way into town with sweat darkening his shirt at the armpits. Deep in thought he crossed the square to Lenny's Pool Hall where he figured there would be air conditioning. Lenny did not go to church and he opened the hall every day.

There were barely a handful of men inside yet the air was clogged with cigar smoke on account of Fats Murphy, a big man with bad teeth who ran the lunch counter but right now was bent over a pool table with a half-smoked stogie clamped in his jaws.

'How you been, Lenny?' Approaching the counter Noble did his best at some kind of conversation though he wasn't noted for making small talk.

'I been kind of hot mostly,' Lenny said eyeing him a little distastefully, 'what with the weather and all. What about you?'

Noble glanced to where Fats worked his pool stick into a head of chalk. 'I been okay, I guess. Can I get me a cup of coffee?'

Lenny reached for the pot on the warmer. 'Working any now then are you?'

Noble made a face. 'Thinking of going after the catfish, see if I can't sell them over at the market; old man Sandling's always after fresh caught fish and they say the river's teeming.'

'Just got out again then did you?' Lenny nodded knowingly. 'All you boys seem to want to head for the water soon as you get clear of the work-house. Need to get you a skiff first I reckon, little old row boat. I got one going cheap if you got the green to cover her.'

He poured the cup of coffee. 'Don't suppose you do though, huh. I mean you ain't been around for a while. Fact is I figure you been up the road so often these past few years they must've gotten you your own set of them jammies special.'

Noble didn't say anything.

'How's that square with your brother,' Lenny went on, 'you being in the workhouse all the time and him being a sheriff's deputy?'

Again Noble didn't answer.

'You living out of that old Pullman are you?'

'That what it is, a Pullman?'

'Sure is, one of the best they ever made and how it wound up side of the track like that I swear I'll never know.' Lenny took a cloth to the counter. 'Been where it's at since the end of the first war and there's been another'n since. Fix her up some and you'll have a place more swanky than most people's homes, I reckon.'

Noble sipped coffee: 'Yeah well; you-all want to move in with me we can work out a deal for the boat maybe.'

Lenny looked at him then as if he'd grown tired of the conversation. 'You here to play pool, it's a quarter for a rack of balls?'

'Don't have me an quarter, Len,' Noble scratched an itch on his arm. 'I got this nickel is all and you need that for the coffee.'

Outside, he had to bunch his eyes to the sunlight. Head down and hands in his overall pockets he walked across the square and drank from the water fountain reserved for white people. He had a molar come loose and it was bothering him, no pain so far but it was waggly and he could work it with his tongue. He had no money for a dentist so if it got any worse he'd have to take the pliers to it like he'd done before.

He stood there for a moment looking at the statue of Light Horse Harry Lee and thinking about Lenny's boat and if there was any way he could raise enough money to lease it for a week or two. He thought about asking his brother and right then a sheriff's cruiser came around the corner. Black and white, Ford Deluxe with a single red light on the roof and the wailers fixed at the door. Chase was behind the wheel and Noble sat down on the bench to wait for him.

His brother swung the cruiser all the way around the square and pulled over. He sat there in his blue uniform with his flat-brimmed hat lying on the passenger seat next to him. He wore the Colt he was issued on his hip and, leaning across the seat, he rolled down the window.

'Noble,' he said. 'You wander about town like that kicking your heels I'll send you up the road for vagrancy.'

'Like you ain't done that just lately,' Noble eyed him distastefully. 'How is it whatever you got going, Chase, I end up in the workhouse? Anyways, I ain't a vagrant. I got me a place to stay.'

'Yeah, I heard how you're squatting in that old Pullman down where the niggers are at.'

Noble turned his face to the sun. 'Giving the family a bad name, am I? You want I should come out and stay at your place instead? I could do that. You remember that invitation you-all give me when I come back from the war? Any day you choose I could go ahead and take you up on her.'

Chase peered at him and Noble peered back, his brother thin in the face, hair shaved at the sides and cut short on top like he had just got out of the army. Only Chase hadn't ever been in the army. All the time there was fighting in Europe he had patrolled the streets of Light Horse County keeping everyone safe in their beds while his brother stormed the beaches of Normandy.

———

Morgan J had not yet left Atlantic City. He had tried to leave his room at the Grand Hotel on the Boardwalk, but Shoofly showed up and he had to suffer a public audience with the black gangster right there in the lobby. Embarrassing as it was, he had no choice but to ride the elevator back to the top floor suite he hadn't paid a buck on in months now.

In his fifties and heavy set, Morgan J had a full head of black hair that was beginning to fleck a little gray. Shoofly was young and dandy; his suit more expensive than Morgan J's, it was double-breasted and tailor-made and the shine on his shoes was so bright a man could see his face in it. Shoofly was thirty years old; he was handsome and the two goons that shouldered him had muscles popping the hand stitched seams of their own suits.

For the first time in his life Morgan J felt shabby; underdone and more than outshone by black men. Back in the day his family had owned men like these who sat so easily on his rented furniture drinking whiskey poured from the cut glass decanter the hotel refilled every day.

He still could not get his head around the fact that Dandy Nichols had sold his note. Maybe he had gotten wind of the fact that his father was no longer picking up his bills and that had made him nervous. He had reminded Dandy that it didn't matter. He told him that as soon as the old man passed away not only would the house on Spanish Bluff be his but Half-Mile-Island as well. That meant it could be developed finally, a marina and a hotel maybe. But Dandy wasn't interested. Dandy told him that fifty thousand dollars was a lot of cash and he could not afford to wait any longer.

Shoofly had bought the debt and Morgan J could tell by his expression how much he was enjoying putting the squeeze on him; not just because he was a white man, but because he was a Barra whose mother had been a McElroy.

Shoofly spoke with a soft voice; dark eyes easy, his lips slack. 'I hate to have to come here like this, Morgan J,' he said, 'but I heard you were leaving out of the place already.'

For a long moment Morgan J just looked at him. Shoofly swallowed the remains of his whiskey and handed the glass to the goon standing next to him.

'You know what,' Morgan J said. 'In another time I wouldn't be set here listening to the likes of you.'

'No sir, you wouldn't. In another time you might've owned the likes of me.' Shoofly nodded then knowingly. 'I know the history. I know who your mama was, I know all about Half-Mile Island and those big old bucks they freighted up from New Orleans because down there black flesh was a whole lot cheaper than it was in Georgia.' His eyes had darkened a little. 'But that was back in the day and we ain't back in the day no longer.'

'I'm good for the money,' Morgan J told him. 'Dandy'll vouch for me. I'm good for everything I owe.'

'Morgan J, Dandy just sold you to me.' Shoofly studied him. 'You talking about your daddy covering what you owe? I heard he ain't as quick to write checks as he used to be.'

A little crimson at the cheeks now Morgan J sat forward. 'Shoofly, have you any idea how much money I'm worth? Everything the old man has comes to me and he's not going to be around much longer. Just this morning I had a call telling me I ought to get down there because he could pass on any day.' Sitting back again he crossed an ankle on his knee. 'Half-Mile Island belongs to me. Think what that would be worth with a marina on it. We're talking water-skiing, shark fishing and blue marlin.' He loosened the knot of his tie. 'I've been working on those plans since I was twenty years old and I figure that with the war over, that place is ripe for development. If I were you I wouldn't be thinking about fifty thousand dollars, I'd be thinking of the profit I could make with that fifty invested.'

On his feet he paced to the window, one hand in his trouser pocket he considered the boardwalk below. The heat was oppressive and it reached right into the room. 'Thing I can't figure is why Dandy wanted out when he did.' He shook his head. 'He knows what I got going and a slice of that action is worth way more than the measly few bucks we're talking. Shoofly, I swear, you stick this out and you can quadruple your money.'

Watching him with his head to one side Shoofly clicked his tongue. 'Fact is I'm a bookmaker not a banker. You want to talk investment best you call a broker.' His eyes dulled now, a chill about them suddenly. 'Don't mess with me, Morgan J. You got seven days to come up with what you owe.'

———

SIX

Gliding across the lagoon to the jetty Pious flipped the kill switch and the motor died. John Q had the rope ready and, jumping out of the boat, he tied it to the cleats fixed to a wooden piling.

Shading a hand to his eyes he gazed the length of the beach. Pious got out and together they stood for a moment.

'Some kind of place, Pious,' John Q gave a low whistle. 'You said how nobody lives here?'

'Not no more they don't. Not for a long time: this whole island is empty and that's six miles long and a half mile wide and there ain't nothing here but hogs and wild horses.'

'What about her?' John Q pointed to the tree lined terraces where he could see Willow watching them with her hip pushed out and a fist resting on it as if they had shown up to spoil her day.

Leading the way up the beach he considered the truculent looking posture and thinking about everything Billy Culpepper had said, he was wondering if this was another one of those smokescreens. If it was he could call her bluff maybe, say something to get her going but he didn't know if he was that confident. It didn't look like a smokescreen and he had no idea how to play those kinds of games anyway. As far he was concerned it looked for all-the-world like they had shown up to spoil her party.

'Hey,' he called a little cautiously. 'How you doing, Willow; are you over here on your own?'

'I was,' she stated. 'Don't you know this is my island?'

'Yours,' John Q lifted his eyebrows. 'You mean the whole place? Wow, I never knew that. What are you some kind of millionaire?'

She glared at him, features taut suddenly. 'I'm talking about my family, my great-grandpa; the island belongs to him right now and....'

'So it ain't yours at all then is it.'

Still she stared at him only now her eyes were darker. She opened her mouth to say something back but then she closed it again and looked hard at Pious.

Pious stood kicking at the dirt. John Q glanced at him and then he turned back to Willow.

'You want us to take off we can do that,' he said. 'But I figured the place was big enough for a couple of people to come visit without upsetting anybody.'

Willow did not say anything so he went on a little awkwardly.

'My grandma was only just telling me how she was the midwife that used to come over to make sure the babies didn't die right after they were born. She told me how the last baby she delivered here was your mom, Willow; who I met by the side of the road.'

At that Willow went red. She stood there with her fist still clenched and her lips a line in her face. Then she swung on her heel and stalked up the path with her back straight and shoulders hunched to her neck.

Watching her, John Q wagged his head at Pious. 'I guess you-all want to be on your own,' he called after her. 'We'll take off. Maybe we'll see you later.'

Willow paused. She looked back over her shoulder. 'No,' she said slowly. 'That's okay; you can stick around now you're here if you want to.'

'Girls,' Pious muttered, 'never could figure them, I swear.'

They started up the hill then with John Q walking ahead. 'Great place this, Willow,' he said, 'your momma must've had some kind of time growing up here. Me, I'd have loved to have been a kid out here. Texas is fine and everything, but a whole island and that swimming tank right there on the beach.' He whistled then softly.

'My grandmother lived here,' Willow considered him now as she spoke. 'This was her home and Friday was the anniversary of when she passed away. Pious,' she said, 'do you know what happened to her?'

Pious shook his head.

'She was drowned in The Pit.' Willow pointed across The Dividing. 'She was driving a car when it wrecked on Bluff Bridge and she went down into that whirlpool. That's where we were going when we had that flat on Friday.'

John Q stared at her. Pious stared at her and Willow stood there with the brooding expression she'd been wearing replaced by one of sadness.

'I'm sorry,' John Q said. 'We didn't know that. We had no idea. I guess you do need to be on your own.'

'No, it's all right.' She looked up again. 'Course you didn't know. I only just met you and there's no reason for Pious to have known.'

'Well,' he gestured. 'We're sorry.'

'I never knew her,' Willow said. 'I went to the bridge with my mother on account of my dad not being able to do it because he's......'

John Q was feeling really awkward now. 'Pious told me your daddy was killed in the war,' he said, 'same as my grandpa was killed in the first one.' He could see how tears were brimming in Willow's eyes suddenly and he stopped talking.

Turning away from them then Willow walked into the trees and kept going until she disappeared from view.

John Q spoke to Pious. 'You know her better than me, bud: you figure she's going to be all right?'

'I don't know,' Pious shrugged. 'Yeah, I reckon she will. Let's just leave her be.'

A few minutes later she was back, the two boys were wandering from cabin to cabin and Willow came up behind them.

'Pious,' she said, 'your mama lived over here when she was a kid didn't she?'

Looking over his shoulder he nodded. 'Yes she did. Told me how there were Indians over here and everything.'

Willow glanced at John Q. 'Mama Sox is our housekeeper.' She spoke to Pious again. 'Did she tell you how Mr Barra said you should probably come and live above the garage now?'

Pious nodded. 'She done said that to me and your mom talked about it yesterday.'

'That's right,' Willow said. 'I forgot you were at the drugstore, weren't you. Well anyway, I think it's all arranged. You know Mr Barra is sick though, don't you?'

Pious nodded.

They were all of them quiet after that and then Willow pointed to a hut which was actually two huts that seemed to have been tacked together. On the second terrace it was shaded by a stand of trees.

'That's where my mother was born,' she said. 'Pious, that's where your mother helped out with her birth.' She looked at John Q. 'It must've been your grandma she was helping.'

'That's what she told me.'

Willow seemed to think about that. Then she smiled for the first time since they had got there. 'So then it's all of us,' she stated, 'we all have something to do with this place, you and me, Pious because of our mothers and you as well, John Q.'

'I guess we do.' John Q liked the way she said his name. He liked the sound of it coming from her lips and now there was that lump in his throat again and his mouth had gone all dry.

Again Willow gestured to the hut. 'I have a picture of my grandma in a locket I got at home. Her name was Laurel and she was very beautiful and my mother doesn't think she was driving that car when it wrecked like everybody said.'

Now John Q stared at her. 'She doesn't?'

'No she doesn't. She never has. On Friday she let me read the piece they wrote in the paper and it said she was drunker than a skunk on moonshine.'

'But she wasn't?'

Willow shook her head. 'Momma says she didn't like to drink at all.'

For a moment John Q thought about that. 'So if it wasn't her driving then who was it?'

Willow shrugged. 'She thinks it might've been Morgan Junior.' As soon as she'd said it she looked as if she knew she should've kept her mouth shut. Biting her lip she turned to Pious. 'Pious,' she said, 'don't you let on you heard me say that. Don't you be telling anyone you heard me say that, not even your mama, you hear?'

Arms across his chest Pious nodded. 'I won't, Miss Willow. I promise.'

'Who's Morgan Junior?' John Q asked.

Neither Willow nor Pious said anything. Willow was looking at Pious and he was staring at the dirt.

'It doesn't matter,' Willow said finally. 'It's not important. It was a long time ago and she never said it was him she just wondered. Anyway,' she added, 'let's just pretend I didn't say anything.'

Changing the subject she headed off down the path. 'Did you know my mother called me after a special tree that grows at Cooper's Bluff? I guess my grandmother was named after a Laurel bush so she thought it would be nice to do that with me. Momma was named after a constellation. Stars,' she turned now and gestured. 'Everybody thinks her name is short for Cassandra or something like that but it's not, it's Cassiopeia.' She pointed to the sky. 'That's a constellation. Did you know that?'

The boys both shook their heads.

Willow seemed more relaxed now and the three of them walked the length of the terrace inspecting each of the cabins in turn. They went down to the lowest level, wandering all the way to the far end where the trees gave out and the sandstone cliff took over. The last cabin was one of the best in the whole settlement with the roof intact and only a slight bow in the walls.

Willow studied it with her head slightly to one side. 'That's Mama Sox's old place, Pious, isn't it?'

'Yes it is.' Pious had his arms folded across his chest. 'It's where my grandma lived at and where my mama was born.'

'It's in pretty good shape,' Willow stepped right up to the door, 'better than most I reckon.'

'Sure is,' John Q followed her. 'Hey,' he said. 'You know what, I'm here for the summer fixing up my grandma's place but I get Sundays off. I got paint and brushes and my grandpa's tools, if you want we could work on this cabin maybe, yours too, Willow: fix them up just like those folks did back when your mothers were kids.'

Willow made a face. 'I don't think that'd be a good idea.'

'No, how's that?'

'I told you my great-grandpa is sick. When he dies the island goes to Morgan J and anything we fix up he's only going to tear down again after.'

———

When he got home that evening Willow was on his mind even more than she had been when he woke up. She was all he could think about and he had a sort of weight in the pit of his stomach and he hadn't experienced that kind of feeling before. The nearest he had known was when his dog died and he'd been pining for weeks. But he liked Willow so why would he be pining? There was something about her that had really gotten to him and all he could figure was that this was how it affected him. He really didn't understand it at all.

They had spent the whole day exploring and he had barely been able to take his eyes off her. She showed them the tree she had been named after and the Sugar Cane Trail and the pond at Yellow Pine. She took them to the Orange Blossom River where she had moored her boat and, from the headland above, she pointed out the salt marsh and the maze-like route through it the islanders had named "The Jabberwock" after some English poem.

John Q's grandmother had made a pot roast for dinner and he sat down to meat and gravy mashed potatoes. He told her about his day and how Willow had been over on the island. He told her how it seemed fixed now that Pious and his sister would go to live above the garage at Spanish Bluff.

'Well I'll tell you,' his grandma said, 'that'd be a whole lot better than where they're at right now. Those god-awful cabins the colored folks have to put up with. Eunice running around on her own all the time Mama Sox is working. That's no good to her. Half the time she's not even in school and if anybody's going to make any kind of something of their life they need to get an education.'

With a sigh then she sat back and folded her hands in her lap. 'So Mr Barra is as sick as they say?'

Wiping his plate with a piece of cornbread John Q nodded. 'Willow told us he ain't got long and she's scared of what might happen on account of Morgan J. I heard a lot about him today, Grandma and he don't sound like the kind of guy anyone would want to be around too long and he sure as hell don't like Willow's mother.'

'No he doesn't.' Pushing back her chair, his grandmother got to her feet. She eased a lock of loose, gray hair behind her ear. 'Come on outside if you're done,' she told him. 'It'll be cool now. I've a mind to smoke some so leave those dishes where they're at and come set with me.'

He followed her out to the porch where a stiff breeze had lifted and sitting in her rocker his grandmother sniffed the air. 'Fixing to rain here in a little bit,' she stated. 'That wind will drop pretty soon and when it starts out raining it don't hardly seem to know how to stop. Folks on low-lying ground can go from hard-baked earth where you need a pick axe to dig a hole to being flooded out in a heartbeat.'

Fumbling for her pipe, she fetched a sack of tobacco from the pocket of her pinafore and shredded some into the bowl. She pressed it down with a thumb.

'Morgan Barra Junior,' she said with a sigh. 'With the old man so sick no doubt he'll be showing up pretty soon.'

'Willow told me he's going to tear down that old slave settlement.' John Q gestured towards the river. 'Over there on the island, she said how he's been fixing to build some kind of marina right where those cribs are at.'

'He's been fixing to do it as long as I can remember,' his grandma told him. 'He's no good, son. I don't mind saying it and I don't mind who hears me either.'

———

SEVEN

That night the rain came just as his grandma had forecast it would and in the morning John Q could hear it hammering on the tin roof which meant he could do no more work on the house. He sat hunched on the stoop with water falling in a gray mist and wondered what he was going to do with his day.

At the same moment Pious was staring out of the window of the apartment above the garage and he still could not believe he was there. Last night when he got home from the island his mama was packed and ready to go. With Eunice holding Pious' hand and all the neighbors looking on, they waited for Albert to swing by in Mr Barra's Cadillac M-24.

It had been his first night in a room of his own; south of the railroad the shack was so small he and his two elder brothers shared a bed while Eunice slept with their mother. Now he had a room to himself, and while Eunice still shared with their mother, it was in a bed of her own.

Pious could not get his head around it. He could not figure that he was actually in this kitchen where the Frigidaire gave off a hum like a bee at a flower and this morning they had cooked pancakes on the gas fired hotplate. The kitchen was large enough for a table and high-backed chairs as well as a couple of easy chairs set around the pot-belly stove.

For the first time in his life they had a roof that did not leak and windows you could see out of and beds with cotton sheets. They had electric light and an inside toilet as well. His mama told him that was only right and proper seeing as how it wasn't that long since the Supreme Court had given black people the right to vote. She told him that if a person could vote for who was running the country they were entitled to a few of its basic amenities. She said the only fly in the ointment was Eugene Talmadge because if he made governor again he had vowed to keep black people in their place.

It had rained all night and it was raining this morning and the way that mist was settled over the bluff right now, Pious figured it would be raining for a couple days at least. His mother was across at the big house together with his sister who was dusting the furniture. Pious had just finished with the grass cuttings and they couldn't do any more in the yard until this rain got quit so Albert told him to go back upstairs. He was thinking that with no work till the rain cleared he should go see what John Q was doing. He liked that kid out of Texas and, with the way the weather was right now, sure as hell he wouldn't be house-painting.

With that thought in his head he went down the stairs that led to the garage. Morgan J had arrived late last night. They said he flew into Candler Field and got the train from Atlanta and Albert had fetched him from the train station in the car.

Outside he heard raised voices; Morgan J and Mr Barra were sitting at table on the patio sheltered from the rain by the upstairs balcony. Pious could smell coffee and cigar smoke and he could see Morgan J with a nasty looking expression on his face. He was smoking a thin cheroot, rolling it between his fingers and inhaling harshly. Next to him the old man looked frailer than he had when he spoke to them yesterday.

Pious watched Morgan J gesticulate with the cigar. Smoke drifted and the old man flapped it away. Then he said something and his eyes were dark and narrow. Like a couple of bulls squaring up they looked at one another with their lips thin and features taut, their noses all but pressed together. Morgan J said something Pious couldn't make out then he got up from the table with the cigar clamped between his teeth and stalked inside. He slammed the door so hard the balcony shook and it was then Pious saw Willow hovering at the rail.

The next thing he knew Albert was beside him with one hand resting on his shoulder. Pious had not heard him come up. He must have walked around the other side of the swimming pool from the kitchen and come in through the workshop door.

'Pious,' Albert said. 'Mama Sox wants flour and sugar from the store. I ain't going to get the car out to run a message like that I got plenty to do around here. You kicking your heels right now on account of this rain I guess you can take the bicycle.'

He cycled into town with the rain falling in stair rods from the sky. Albert gave him an oilskin to keep him dry, a yellow cape with wire in the hood like the Atlantic fishermen wear. It was way too big for him, reaching right over the handlebars it came down as low as his knees and did keep off most of the water. He had seen his mother ride this bicycle, a roadmaster with a rack over the back wheel and a basket fixed for the groceries. He had that covered by the oilskin right now and he had a dollar bill folded in his pocket. His mother told him to go see Mr Telling at the grocery store. She told him how the Barra's had an account of course, but she had not had time to tell the storekeeper that her family was moving up to the Bluff so he better have cash money with him.

He cycled the dirt road thinking on what he had seen go down just now between Mr Barra and Morgan J and how Willow seemed to have been listening. He had not seen Mrs Flood at all this morning and figured she must've gone out early. There was no sign of the convertible and he was thinking about that when another automobile whooshed past almost knocking him into the trees.

When he got to town he spotted the car again parked outside Murphy's Lunch Counter. The grocery store was across the road and he leaned the bicycle against the wall. Still the rain fell hard and there was nobody much about and none of the old men were sitting under the canopy. There were no chairs on the sidewalk at all. Leaving the bicycle, Pious fished in his pocket for the money.

There was only the one door into the store, but there were two queues one at each end of the counter the one for coloreds marked clearly with a sign. He had been in here many times to fetch groceries for his mother and he knew where the flour was at and reached for that and a bag of sugar.

Mrs Telling was serving and Pious told her how he was living up at the Bluff now and how he might be down here on a regular basis and Mrs Flood would send word so he didn't have to carry cash dollars. Inspecting him from the other side of the counter, Mrs Telling said that was fine but she would wait until she heard from Mrs Flood; meantime he owed twenty seven cents for the packages.

Outside he packed them into the basket, but instead of fixing the oilskin and heading back to the Bluff he stared across the road. The glass at Murphy's window was misted with condensation but he could see Morgan J in his gray suit and white shirt, jacket hanging over the chair. It had been his car that almost knocked Pious off the bicycle and he was sitting there on his own wearing the same heated expression Pious had witnessed at the house. The waitress came over in her candy-striped outfit and little paper hat and she poured him a cup of coffee. If Morgan J saw her he did not acknowledge it, he just sat there smoking his cigar.

Pious turned back to his bicycle and was fitting the oilskin cape when a car came around the corner, a black and white sheriff's prowl car with the red light on the roof and Peyton Skipwith driving. Next to him was Chase Landry whose brother had just got out of the workhouse. Pious watched as they went into Murphy's and sat down across the table from Morgan J. He saw Morgan J crush his cigar in the ashtray and spoon sugar into his coffee. He seemed to take a good long look at the two deputies, then scan the diner to see who might be eavesdropping. Then as if he were satisfied they were not being overheard, Pious saw him lean across the table.

——

John Q was still sitting on the stoop. He had offered to do some work inside the house but his grandma told him it was only the outside she wanted fixing up. After fifty years living there she had only just managed to get the inside how she liked it and did not need him messing with it.

He was about to cross to the workshop when he saw Pious cycle up the road smothered in a yellow oilskin. 'Hey, bud,' he called, 'what you doing?'

Pious climbed off the bicycle. He wheeled it up the path and John Q helped him with the cape. 'Can you believe this rain,' he said, 'fixing to come down for about a week already according to what my grandma was telling me.'

'Can be like that around here,' Pious took shelter on the porch. 'I seen it before plenty times before.' He held out a palm. 'No wind or anything, air just still as the grave, that's when it can rain and rain and rain. I figure your grandma's right, could be set like this for days.' He worked a hand across his tightly curled hair. 'Figure you ain't doing any house painting though, so what else you got going on?'

'Not a whole lot as it goes.' John Q was quiet for a moment. He looked at Pious and at the bicycle then his eyes lit up and he indicated across the yard to the workshop. 'Found something yonder might interest you. Come on over and I'll show you, okay?'

Inside the workshop, he closed the door then bent to the bench and withdrew a long wooden box from the shelf underneath. The lid was screwed down at each corner and he worked the four screws loose and lifted the lid right off. Inside the box was packed tightly with straw and when he lifted that out Pious could see a slender package of wax paper.

With his tongue poking over his lips now, John Q lifted the package and began to unravel the paper. Inside was the most beautiful lever action rifle Pious had ever seen.

'That's a seventy-three Winchester right there.' John Q laid the gun down on the work bench then wiped his hands on his thighs. 'The way they tell it that's the rifle that won the west and I only seen one like her before: seen a few of the '94 model, but they were a thirty-thirty. This is the forty-four-forty, Pious; one of the first to be made out of Newhaven, Connecticut, says so on the box right there. I tell you, you look at this piece you can see she ain't hardly ever been fired.'

Lifting the gun now he smoothed a palm over the breech before working the hammer back gently with his thumb. 'Got her a safety notch, see that? Safety notch and full cock; ain't barely a mark on the metalwork. See how that is right there? That's how I know she ain't been fired. Grandma told me it belonged to her daddy and he fought in the civil war. Used a musket back then most likely or a Henry maybe if he could get a-hold of one. If that'd been me it'd be the Henry I'd prefer.' He sounded very authoritative. 'Grandma told me he bought this when they first come out though. Look at the box, Pious: "Winchester Repeating Arms Company" that's what it says right there.'

Pious' eyes were like saucers now and, with reverence almost, he ran the points of his fingers over the barrel of the gun.

'She's a beauty, John Q,' he said. 'I don't know nothing about rifles, I ain't never fired one, but she looks real nice and I seen one like this in the movies a couple of years back, that picture they done with John Wayne.'

'"Tall in the Saddle" you're talking,' John Q nodded. 'Yeah, I saw that. Listen, bud, I kind of figured we'd take her over to the island sometime maybe and see if we can't bag us a hog.' Standing back then he squinted. 'You ain't ever fired a rifle, huh? Well, I can teach you, Pious; see if you ain't some kind of shot.'

Carefully he re-wrapped the weapon in the waxed paper and placed it back in the box.

'Need to get a dollar together for some ammo first though,' he stated. 'I'll ask Grandma if she's got any but I can't see none around here.'

Pious re packed the straw. '1873, you say?'

'Uh-huh.'

'So that makes her about.....'

'It makes her seventy-three years old,' John Q stated. 'I worked it out already. Seventy-three years for the '73 Winchester. Bud, there's got to be something in that, some kind of omen for sure.'

Closing the lid he re-screwed the corners and replaced the box on the shelf then indicated the wall where an old loop of catch rope was hanging.

'See that,' he stated. 'That was in the trunk of our car the last time we were here, brought it out from Texas by mistake. We drove over for Christmas after Pearl Harbor got hit like I told you and nobody knew the rope was in the car. Never took it back I guess. Grandma hung it here on account of what else was she going to do with it and I seen it the other day.' Now he gestured. 'We can take the Winchester when we got ammo but how's about we cross the water right now and see if I can't get a loop on one of those horses.'

Doubtfully, Pious looked from him to the rope and back again.

'You ever rope a wild horse, Pious?' John Q asked him.

'No I didn't; never fired no gun and I never roped a horse neither; wouldn't know how.'

'I got a way with them.' John Q puffed out his chest now. 'Folks think I like to brag on it and everything, but it ain't like that. Fact is I worked three summers with Billy Culpepper's dad and he breeds cutting horses.'

'What's a cutting horse?' Pious asked him.

'Those that work up close with the cattle. They can turn real quick, cut a steer from the herd and keep it from getting back. If you seen a Winchester in the movies like you said then you probably seen a cutting horse too.'

He found an oilskin in the closet in the basement and slipped it on. Pious had his already and protected against the rain, they headed down to the landing.

'I was going to tell you,' Pious said as they untied the boat. 'I was in town just now and I saw Morgan J at the lunch counter. He was setting with Chase Landry and Peyton Skipwith, those deputies I told you about.'

Pausing with the rope in his hand John Q wrinkled his brow. 'Morgan Junior that Willow was talking about - what's he want with sheriff's deputies?'

'Beats me, but they was talking, John Q and it looked like some kind of pow wow going on right there.' Pious spread a palm. 'That ain't all. Right before that happened I was up at the big house and Morgan J was set there on the patio arguing with his daddy. I don't know what it was about but they were going at it and I saw Willow up on the balcony like she was listening to every word.'

They headed for the Dividing and the tides seemed quiet as they approached the bay. Pious was navigating of course, though John Q sat in the stern with him this time to watch where he made the turns.

'Pretty good in boat ain't you,' he stated, 'told Grandma it ain't my thing.'

'I ain't never roped no horse before, did I, and I never shot a rifle.' Pious nodded to the catch rope. 'Looking forward to seeing what you can do with that thing. If you get a loop on one of them mustangs are you fixing to ride?'

'I don't know,' John Q thought about that. 'Might-could be I guess; been on wild ones before though, Pious and mostly they bucked me off.'

They were not the only ones on the river in the rain. Halfway between the landing and the shoals they spotted a fisherman laying a series of lines. Noble Landry piloting a row boat, briefly he looked their way.

'Catfish, I reckon, most likely,' Pious stated. 'Fetch more money than a bugle mouth, but Mr Sandling going to buy 'em either way.' He gestured further upriver. 'Head thataway a mile or so and there's houseboats all along the shore, lines everywhichwhere, tied off to rubber tires most of 'em, can't hardly paddle for getting tangled up I swear.'

As they crossed the channel, he pointed out the dorsal fin of a shark where it broke the surface about fifty feet from the boat. 'Sumbuck right there, John Q: bull shark and a big one at that. Don't suppose you get many of those back in Texas, do you.'

John Q was on his feet so he could see better and the boat rocked horribly. For one awful moment he thought he was going over and with a cry he grabbed for the gunwale.

'Set down will you,' Pious yelled at him. 'Goddamnit, you don't do that in a boat. Stood up like that you'll be tipping us over and then where would we be?'

John Q sat down heavily beside him. Still he held the side of the boat and he was shaking as the shark came alongside.

'I swear,' Pious told him, 'you ride in a boat with me you set tight unless I tell you different. You fall in then probably you ain't coming out again and I sure as hell ain't coming in to get you.'

'Do they go upriver?' Sitting there recovering from the fright John Q was staring as the shark swam away.

'Bull Shark,' Pious looked sideways at him, 'sure they do; fresh water don't seem to bother them like it does other sharks and they get right on in where it's shallow, seen them paddling on their bellies almost and when they do that you best be out of the water you want to keep your toes.'

They made it to the lagoon finally, and, as they approached the jetty, they saw Willow's boat already tied up. They could see her up on the terrace keeping out of the rain and as John Q secured the line he waved to her and this time she waved back.

———

EIGHT

Sitting in the booth at the lunch counter Morgan J lit another cigar. Across the table Chase Landry had his hat upturned and his gun hunched round on his hip. Next to him Peyton Skipwith slouched as Peyton always did. The waitress came by with the coffee pot and Morgan J fell silent as she refilled his cup.

'Can I get you anything else, Mr Barra?' she asked him.

'No, coffee's good.'

'What about you two officers?'

'Coffee's fine,' Chase echoed and flapped his hand to wave her away.

When she was gone he hunched with his elbows on the table and looked across at Morgan J. With the weather as it was right now the counter was very busy and Morgan Barra's son being in town was a novelty so everybody looked their way. Mindful of eaves-droppers Chase spoke in a whisper. 'So he told you all this just now?'

Morgan J nodded. 'Got to Candler Field yesterday and caught the train out. Didn't see the old man till this morning and he was pretty damn frail I tell you.' His eyes were narrow. 'Not lost any of his bile though and it didn't stop him hitting me with the news right off, told me it was done and dusted and there wasn't a damn thing I could do about it.'

'But why,' Peyton gestured. 'I don't get it, what with your mother and all?'

Morgan J sat back now with a fist bunched on the table in front of him. 'I don't know, Peyton: there's no accounting for foolish old men and my mother's been gone a long time. It never mattered that she was a McElroy, the old man's old school proper and he's always done things his way.' He worked the cigar between his fingers. He looked from one deputy to the other. 'Goes back twenty years I reckon, right back to that time I was in the hospital after Laurel Brown wrecked that Ford in The Pit.' The expression in his eyes tightened then at the memory. 'You remember that, Peyton? You were in the parking lot when the old man swung by.'

It was a couple of days since the automobile had crashed and Peyton had driven from Spanish Fork to the hospital at Rutherford the county seat. He was outside in the parking lot about to climb behind the wheel of the sheriff's Ford when Mr Barra turned off the road.

A little nervously Peyton waited, knowing the old man had spotted him and aware that he could not just take off without acknowledging him. Mr Barra parked right next to him and climbing from his automobile he was wearing a business suit and black tie.

Standing up straight Peyton checked to make sure all his buttons were fastened before hitching up the gun where it lolled at his side.

'Mr Barra,' he tipped a forefinger to his hat. 'How are you, sir?'

The old man's gaze was icy. 'I've been better, Deputy,' he said. 'Just come from the memorial service actually. They tell me it was you who was first on the scene.'

'Yes sir, I was.'

'You were just driving that road by chance then?'

Peyton shook his head. 'No sir; I'd been in town on account of a tip-off we'd had that alcohol was being served someplace along the highway. Didn't turn out that way, only booze on the market that night was corn mash and I saw that squatter cross the street looking pretty loaded. Saw her jump in that Ford just like it said in the newspaper.'

Mr Barra half-closed one eye: 'You saw her drive off all liquored up as she was?'

Peyton gestured. 'Sir, she's a squatter, pilots a boat across The Dividing most every day. That old crank ain't a problem, not for a woman like that.'

The old man looked closely at him. 'And my son was in the cafe?'

'Yes sir he was.'

'How'd she get the key?'

'Excuse me?'

'To the Ford: how did the squatter get hold of the key?'

Peyton colored. 'Mr Morgan told me he left the key in the car, sir, all she had to do was crank the handle.'

'No she didn't, she had to set the spark is what she had to do. After that she had to prime the throttle just right and then she had to walk around the front and crank the handle. With a Model T that's one half turn and you have to get it just right otherwise it's going to spring back on you.' Mr Barra peered at him now. 'She had to do all that, Deputy; and from what you're telling me hog-whimpering drunk on shine.'

Morgan J stared across the lunch room where the other diners did not register. 'He came to see me right after,' he stated, 'didn't give a damn how I was all busted up, he just told me about that conversation he'd had with you, Peyton and what he thought about it. Seeing as how he'd been to the funeral I figured he was just blowing off.' He looked back at the deputies then. 'But he wasn't of course was he.'

'That's a fact,' Chase said with a sigh. 'So this business now though, what all he told you: what're we going to do about that?'

Lip curled Morgan J studied him. 'Chase,' he said. 'We're going to take care of that squatter like we took care of her mother. Cassie and her daughter we're going to deal with them once and for all.'

———

Feeling a little forlorn now John Q stood in the doorway to Willow's mother's old cabin. He was holding the coiled catch rope but the rain was coming down even harder than it had been when they were crossing the shoals and the two colts he had spotted when he walked up the beach had long since taken off.

'Couldn't get close,' he was saying. 'Have to come back maybe, try for it another day.'

'When it's not raining,' with a nod Willow moved next to him, the top of her head barely reaching to his shoulder. He could smell the moisture in her hair and he had that same ache in his belly again and it was bothering him even more. He had never been this way around a girl before, not even Betty Moore and they had been seeing each other for a year.

They had followed the colts a good way along the beach and Pious had told Willow what John Q planned to do and he was a little gutted he had not been able to show her.

Moving from under the eaves Willow stepped outside where the mist hung like a soaking curtain.

'Do you want to explore some more?' she asked. 'No sense in us being over here if we don't put some kind of use to it.'

'I guess not,' John Q glanced at Pious. 'What say, bud: you fancy taking another walk in the rain?'

Pious shrugged. 'Why not; guess we ain't quite wet enough yet are we.'

They left the settlement and made their way up the muddy hill with Willow taking the lead as she had done yesterday. She kept to the larger rocks so she would not lose her footing and the two boys trod where she did. At the top of the hill the ground levelled onto a sort of escarpment and beyond the trees another pathway took off through a sea of long grass. Yesterday they had gone south from here and explored that part of the island. Right now they were up in the northwest and Willow said that this was one of two places where the island was at its widest.

'The other is at Cooper's Bluff,' she explained, 'where that tree was I showed you yesterday.' Easing the sleeve back on the oilskin where it was too big for her, she pointed.

'Go north or east from here and we hit the Atlantic proper, before that is the McElroy Mansion at High Point. D'you want to check that out?'

She explained how the mansion had been home to the McElroy family who had travelled from Ireland with just about nothing and created a cotton and sugar cane empire that had just about everything. It was a sprawling colonial style building with verandas and balconies and pillars out front all made from live oak that had been cut from the island. Now the wood was rotten and the whole place overgrown with ivy and yellow jasmine. Willow said how sometimes bees mistook the jasmine for nectar and if they carried any back to the hive it would kill every last one of the larvae.

The old road that led up to the place was overgrown and clustered with weeds but the wagon ruts were so deep they were just about still visible. Lining either side of the trail was a series of small huts reminiscent of those at the settlement. Willow said that the slaves who worked in the house had lived in them and there was another village in the valley below. There was a church there too, one of the oldest black churches in America.

'Used to be bears over here as well,' she added. 'My mom says folk reckoned they could smell the corn from the mainland and they'd swim the shoals despite the sharks and everything. She told me a story about one slave who was walking home in the dark one night when he heard a neighbor padding along right behind. He stopped to see who it was only it wasn't a neighbor it was a bear. That slave took off running for his life but the bear was only after the corn he was carrying.'

'Which he dropped I guess then, didn't he?' Pious suggested.

Willow glanced at him with a smile. 'I sure would, wouldn't you?'

John Q was gazing at the house which was pretty ramshackle and weather beaten but still looked spectacular. An old style plantation place, like some he had seen from the window of the bus as he crossed Louisiana on his way from Texas. The roof was sagging at one end but it was intact and out front he could still see the turning circle that had been built for carriages. He could smell corn and what he figured was sugar cane growing wild and he tried to imagine bears swimming The Dividing with bull sharks taking chunks out of them. A bear could take on pretty much anything but not a bull shark and not in open water.

Together they walked the length of that avenue, he and Willow side by side with Pious a few paces behind. Out front of the house Willow paused. Standing with her hand fisted on her hip as before, she indicated a battered sign that hung above those doors that once upon a time had been blue but had faded from years of decline. All the while the rain still fell on their shoulders, the three of them in yellow oilskins; the water trickling into puddles that formed at their feet. They could just about make out what was written.

"KEEP OUT - THIS PROPERTY IS CONDEMNED"

Vehemently now Willow gestured. 'Pious,' she said, 'your mama told me how Morgan J hung that sign back when she was a little girl. Did it to make sure everybody in the village knew just who owned this place and how the huts they lived in didn't belong to them and it was all going to be torn down. I tell you what, if this was my island I'd fix up that house and live in it.'

'You would?' John Q glanced at her.

'Sure I would, a big house like that; a whole island to myself. I'd have carpenters or whatever come over and fix it up and live here and nobody would be building any marina for sailboats or anything.'

She nodded then as if to affirm it. 'I'd have the place to myself, might even fix up the cabins over at the lagoon just like when my mom was a kid.' Eyes hooded slightly she looked sideways at Pious. 'Your mama grew up here, Pious,' she said. 'How'd it be if I fixed up her old place? I reckon you'd like that, wouldn't you?'

'Yes'm, I sure would but only if I could come and visit.'

'Course you could. You too, John Q: your grandma was the midwife so I'd give you a cabin and we'd fix that one up as well.' She fell silent then and turned again to Pious. 'You know Morgan J came home last night, Albert drove to the station and fetched him.'

'Yes'm,' he nodded, 'seen him with Mr Morgan right after I got done with the grass this morning.'

'On the patio there - sitting under the balcony?' Her brows were furrows suddenly. 'You saw that?'

Pious looked evenly at her. 'I saw them talking, didn't hear what-all was said or anything but they didn't seem none too happy.'

Willow looked from him to John Q and then she stared into space momentarily. She seemed to ponder still as she wandered away a few paces. Finally she turned and now her eyes were shining. 'Listen,' she said. 'If I tell you something you have to promise me you'll keep it secret.'

———

NINE

Noble Landry caught a whole stack of bugle mouth but no catfish and it was catfish that brought in the money. Mooring the row boat he had leased from Lenny at the pool hall, he strung the bass and walked through the rain back to town.

The market hall was still open and he stepped inside and paced the tiled floor past the meat counter where a side of pig was set between lunch meats and cuts of beef, whole chickens with their legs tied beneath them. Across the way Bill Sandling the fish-seller had his stall set up and he offered twelve cents on the pound for the Bugle mouth. It wasn't a whole lot and he said he would pay more for catfish and that next time Noble ought to bring catfish.

'Next time', Noble echoed and watched as the fishmonger weighed the catch then peeled two dollars from his money clip and counted out some change. He did not have any pennies and when Noble said he could not split a nickel Sandling cursed softly before handing him sixty five cents instead of the sixty-two he owed.

'Difference'll come off the next batch you bring me,' he stated. 'Here every day. Right now I could do with catfish but I guess I'll take bugles if that's all you can manage. Heard how you were living down there by the railroad, Noble. Mama Sox done moved up to the bluff so there's a nigger cabin going if you want it.' With a grin he tossed the fish in the box and shovelled a handful of ice across them.

Noble left the market and walked past the bus arcade where the announcer was telling everybody that the service to Columbus was about to get going. Crossing the street he avoided Murphy's Lunch Counter and went to a place further down that served coloreds as well as whites and he took a seat at the end of the counter.

He ordered sausage and country gravy, cornbread and cabbage greens. He ordered a glass of milk and the platter was set on the counter before him with a knife and fork and napkin. He passed over a dollar and watched as the waitress counted twenty-six cents in change. Shovelling that into his overall pocket, he settled down to eat. The cornbread was mushy rather than crumbly, but the cabbage was OK. The gravy tasted of meat at least and it helped digest the glutinous nature of the sausage.

When he was done he bought a sack of cigarette tobacco and helped himself to some match books and stood outside in the rain. What he needed was a drink and knew where he could get one without having to head on out to see Willy. During the prohibition years Koontz wasn't the only guy in town who sold liquor and over at the pool hall Lenny kept a few Mason jars under his counter.

———

TEN

As John Q and Pious climbed the steps from the landing the rain was falling even more heavily. Heading towards dusk now, they crossed the yard and spotted Willow's mother's car parked in front of the lean-to. It was then Pious remembered why he had come out in the first place. Flour and sugar, the packages were still in the basket on the bicycle and he had been gone all day. More than a little panicked suddenly, he grabbed the bicycle and headed home.

Watching him pedal off John Q hung the oilskin in the workshop where it could drip dry without making a mess of everything. Crossing the yard once more he could see through the kitchen window where his grandma and Willow's mother were sitting at the table.

After they had explored the McElroy mansion Willow told them she did not think her mother was aware of what had gone on between Morgan J and his father. She didn't see how she could be because she had driven to Rutherford first thing that morning and hadn't spoken to either of them. Willow said she still wasn't sure she had heard right and was trying to figure out what it would actually mean. As they climbed into their boats to come home she had told them they were not to say a word to anyone.

With the wind picking up quite a bit now John Q went into the house through the back porch and as he pushed the door open he heard the conversation from the kitchen fall away. Taking off his boots he slapped them together to get all the mud off then he set them down and closed the outside door. When he went into the kitchen his grandma and Mrs Flood were still at the table and his grandma looked up with a smile.

'Johnny,' she said, 'you met Mrs Flood I think, didn't you?'

'Yes ma'am, I helped Pious fix her flat tire.' Crossing to the table he shook hands. 'How are you, Mrs Flood? It's nice to see you.'

'Nice to see you too, John Q,' she said. 'I told you how I'd visit with your grandma and now I'm here I don't know why it's been so long.' She looked beyond him to the rain that littered the window. 'This weather looks like it's hanging around now, could be raining for days.' She glanced at Grandma Q. 'Having said that, just this lunchtime I was over in Rutherford and there wasn't a single cloud in the sky.'

'Figure she must be hugging to the coast, ma'am,' John Q suggested. 'The rain I mean. I know how a storm can hook up to a mountain and all back in Texas, I figure maybe it's the same with the coast. Sea's calm though, I know that on account of I just got back from Half-Mile Island.'

'You did?' Mrs Flood studied him carefully.

'Yes, ma'am; took the skiff over there with Pious and he sure knows how to shuttle those tides.' He turned to his grandmother then. 'Spotted a bull shark, Grandma; it was headed for the mouth of the river.'

At that Mrs Flood's eyes narrowed. 'Bull shark's do that sometimes,' she told him. 'If you see one actually in the river make sure you tell somebody real quick because children swim the shallows all the time.' She paused then with her head to one side. 'You were with Pious you say? Last I heard that boy was supposed to be running errands for his mother.'

'Yes ma'am,' John Q smiled now, 'he showed up here with some packages. Clean forgot about them I guess. It was my idea to cross to the island and probably that's what distracted him.'

'Well, no doubt he'll feel the knotted end of his mother's dish cloth because of it,' Mrs Flood told him. 'Mama Sox doesn't like to be let down, not when it's a cake she's baking.'

'No ma'am. Willow was over there with us,' he went on, 'she sure likes that place, doesn't she?'

'Yes she does.' Mrs Flood got to her feet now. 'Did she make the crossing back when you did?'

John Q nodded.

'Good. She'll be home then already. I should go and see how she is.' Mrs Flood took his grandma's hands and kissed her on both cheeks. 'So nice to catch up, Mrs Q: so glad we were able to chat some.'

––––

When Willow got home she climbed the wooden steps and crossed the lawn and there was a car she did not recognise parked in the driveway. Something was wrong; she could hear Mama Sox in the house absolutely beside herself. Rushing inside she found her crying her eyes out. In the hallway the door to her great-grandpa's study was open and both the doctor and a nurse were bent to where he lay on the couch.

Willow was frightened suddenly. Heart in her mouth she stepped closer, not knowing what had happened and Mama Sox too upset to explain. But the old man was laid out in his study with the doctor administering something to him while Albert was setting up a bed.

As she stood in the doorway her great-grandpa seemed to look through rather than at her as if he couldn't get his eyes to focus properly. He was lying with one arm dangling and his fingers bunched in a crooked fist. Willow could see how his mouth hung open and his gaze seemed full of fear. She did not know if he could see her or not, but all at once he had a kind of light in his eyes and he seemed to focus and she had the strangest sensation that not only could he see her, in fact he was trying to beckon. She tried to cross the room to get to him but the nurse stepped in her way.

Upstairs in her room Willow sat on the floor with the doors to the balcony wide open. She heard a car pull in and when she got up she saw her mother's convertible by the garage doors.

Downstairs Mama Sox was still crying and as her mother came in Willow was on the landing. Her mother didn't see her and, through her tears, Mama managed to tell her that Mr Barra had had a stroke. She had taken some coffee to his study where she found him lying on the floor.

Leaning on the banister Willow called down. 'Momma, I need to talk to you. I...'

'Give me a minute, Willow,' her mother looked up. 'I've just gotten home and I have to see to grandpa.'

With that she ushered Mama Sox back to the kitchen and went into the study. A couple of minutes later she was back in the hall though, with the doctor and they sat down on the couch.

Willow listened to what was said from where she still hovered on the landing.

'Mr Barra has suffered a stroke,' the doctor explained, 'it was caused by a blood clot most probably and if he wasn't so sick already I would've called an ambulance to take him to Rutherford.'

'But surely he needs the hospital.'

'He does,' the doctor confirmed, 'but it's almost thirty miles and the road's not great and I fear it's going to storm. The journey would probably kill him and we can't risk that, Mrs Flood.' He was quiet for a moment and then he said. 'The problem is he needs some specific drugs that I don't have in Spanish Fork. The stroke is bad and his condition is compounded by his cancer. Right now he's paralysed down one side and he can't speak. We cannot risk an ambulance but he needs those drugs to keep his blood thin because without them it might clot again and I believe a second stroke would finish him.'

———

Morgan J was in Spanish Fork, sitting in the back of the sheriff's prowl car with Peyton Skipwith at the wheel. They were parked in a quiet street close to the railroad tracks and a few minutes earlier Chase had got out and walked the short distance to where his brother had gone back to the Pullman.

En route from the diner, Noble had bought a small hurricane lamp and a can of kerosene from the Mercantile. He was down to his last few cents again but had agreed with Lenny that he would have the boat for a week and would pay him the rest of what he owed when he'd caught some catfish. He had spent most of what he had earned today already and would hit the river again at dawn.

Inside the railroad car he set the hurricane lamp on the table between the only two seats that were left. Taking a drink from the Mason jar he looked up to see his older brother in the doorway.

'What're you doing here, Chase?' Noble asked him.

For a moment Chase just seemed to study him. Then he cast his gaze about the place with his arms folded across his chest and his lip twisted at the corner. Noble looked where he did, considering again how he had created a living area with the two old seats and the table set between them and the way he had positioned a tick of a mattress on the floor in the space behind. The mattress had come from the city dump and had a hole in one corner but not too much of the stuffing had gone missing. He had a rolled up coat for a pillow and a blanket he had traded for with the rag picker.

'Chase,' he said. 'What-all are you doing here?'

His brother lifted his gaze from the soiled surroundings. 'Need to talk to you, Noble. You owe me money right now on account of that boat and it could be I got a job for you.'

———

Willow heard Morgan J arrive home a few minutes after the doctor had left. Her mother had already driven off to Rutherford again and Willow was in the kitchen when the big car rumbled up the driveway.

Mama Sox was still wiping away tears and muttering to herself and she barely noticed when Pious came in with the packages he was supposed to have fetched that morning. Willow glanced at Pious and he glanced at her and when he went over to the garage she followed.

'Do you understand what's happened?' She stood just inside the garage doors where the big black car was clicking and steaming from the rain drops that pooled on the body.

'With Mr Barra,' Pious shook his head. 'I knowed he was sick and everything, but Mama says they's been a doctor up at the house just now and how he ought to be in the hospital.' He upturned his palms. 'She ain't told me what-all's wrong with him.'

'He's had a stroke,' Willow said.

Pious looked blank. 'Miss Willow, I don't know what that is.'

'It's something to do with his brain,' Willow wasn't sure herself; she was only repeating what she had heard the doctor tell her mother, 'something to do with blood getting to it, or not getting to it maybe, some kind of blockage. Anyway, he can't talk and he can't move and Pious.......' she felt a sob rise suddenly. 'I saw him just now and he was looking at me like he had to tell me something.'

'Tell you what?' Pious asked her.

She flapped a hand. 'That's just it; I don't know and now he can't talk so I don't suppose I'll ever know, will I?' Another sob took her: 'Maybe it was to do with what I told you over on the island. I don't know, but I can't get in his study because Morgan J showed up and my mother's gone to get some medicine and I haven't had a chance to say anything.'

———

Inside the house Morgan J closed the door to his father's room and for a moment he just stood there with his back to the wood. His father peered at him where one side of his face had fallen so the eye was partially closed and a line of saliva broke from the corner of his mouth. Morgan J did not take a cloth to it. Instead he closed the doors to the patio where the wind had started blowing. Then he sat down in a chair. For a long time he looked at his father and the old man looked at him.

Morgan J made a steeple of his fingers. 'So how're you feeling?'

Of course his father could not answer.

Getting up again Morgan J crossed to the drinks cart and poured a glass of bourbon.

'Kentucky Straight,' he held the glass up to the light. 'I'd build you one only you'd need a straw to drink it now wouldn't you.' Swallowing a mouthful he inspected the glass once more. 'A stroke, huh. Paralysed down one side; can't hardly see; can't talk, can't do anything much at all anymore can you.' A smile played about his lips now. 'Guess that changes everything.'

———

ELEVEN

Pious cycled all the way back to Riverview Road. It was dark now; raining hard still and John Q's grandma had gone to bed early to read her book. John Q was in the kitchen listening to the radio with his great-grandfather's Winchester on the table in pieces so he could clean and oil it. Pious came around back of the house to where he could see the light burning and lightly he tapped on the window.

John Q beckoned him and Pious came in and sat down at the table. 'I got to talk to you,' he said. 'I got to talk to you about Mr Barra.'

John Q started to put the gun back together. 'Pious,' he said, 'can you believe Grandma only went and told me I can have this rifle; said that as long as I take care of her properly I can keep her.' He was grinning from ear to ear. 'Said I might need her if I'm working up in the panhandle and the fact is Winchester didn't make her just so she could set in wax paper.'

Pious nodded slowly. 'That's real nice,' he said. 'But listen, I come over here to tell you how Mr Barra's had a stroke or something.'

Sitting back now John Q stared at him.

'Can't talk and can't move or nothing. Willow swears he was trying to tell her something.'

Still John Q stared at him. 'Willow sent you?'

Pious nodded. 'She wanted that I come fetch you.'

Quickly now John Q finished reassembling the rifle then went down the hall and knocked on his grandmother's door.

'Grandma,' he said. 'I'm going out for while if that's all right with you?'

'That's all right with me,' she called back. 'Only don't be waking me up when you get home, you hear?'

'No ma'am, I won't. I promise.'

They had to ride two-up on the bicycle; John Q pedalling with Pious sitting on the handlebars. They rode all the way back down Riverview Road then turned toward town with oak trees crowding them like a line of old men hunched against the rain in the darkness.

'So what is it Willow thinks Mr Barra was looking to say to her?' John Q asked.

'She don't know. She never got to talk to him and he can't talk at all now so she figures she'll never know.'

'Might be he could make her understand what he wants some other way,' John Q suggested.

'Might be he could, but she has to get in that study first and Morgan J just kicked everybody out of there. I guess it must be something to do with what-all she overheard.'

'I guess,' John Q said. 'I mean why else would he want to be talking to her?'

'Maybe he knowed she was up there.' Pious flapped a hand. 'Could be that after Morgan J took off slamming doors like that Mr Barra heard Miss Willow on the balcony.'

As they cycled across the square they were spotted by Chase and Peyton sitting in their prowl car. The two deputies, they climbed out as John Q came pedalling beyond the statue.

'Hey, you boy: stop.' Peyton called out and Pious craned his neck right around to see him.

'That's Deputy Skipwith, John Q,' he said, 'best do what he's telling you.'

Working his feet back on the pedals John Q brought the bicycle to a stop and Pious jumped off.

Tramping over to them from the prowl car the deputies shone their flashlights in John Q's face.

'Doubled up with a nigger,' Chase said, 'what the hell do you think you're doing?'

John Q had to squint against the light from the torches. 'Sir,' he said. 'Where I live at there ain't any law against two people being on a bicycle.'

The two deputies exchanged a glance then Peyton took hold of John Q roughly by the shoulder. 'You're the kid out of Texas people been talking about, Grandma Quarrie's boy.'

'I ain't her boy, sir,' John Q told him. 'My daddy's her boy. I'm her grandson.'

Peyton cuffed him with the back of his hand. 'You want to watch that lip, sonny; nobody likes a smart mouth. You ain't in Texas, this here's Georgia and if you're going to stick around any best you learn how we talk to people.' He looked beyond John Q then to Pious. 'I don't know what you think you're doing,' he told him. 'Maybe now you moved up to the Bluff you got the kind of airs and graces lets you think you can hang around with white folks.'

'No, sir,' Pious said.

'What's that? No sir, is that what you said?'

'Yes sir.'

'Yes sir, no sir, you do got them airs and graces, is that what you're telling me?'

'No sir.'

'So what're you doing then? What you doing on the back of that bicycle?'

'He ain't doing anything,' John Q said. 'I'm giving him a ride home on account of the rain is all. Pious, he ain't doing nothing.'

Peyton ignored him. Leaning close he spoke once more to Pious. 'Boy, unless you want the kind of pistol-whipping I used to give your daddy, best you cut along.'

Pious ducked around the corner leaving John Q still sitting on the bicycle. Arms crossed on his chest now he eyed the two deputies.

'Now you-all listen up,' Peyton had hold of the handlebars, the rain falling down and Chase standing back with the heel of his hand resting on the butt of his pistol. There was nobody else on the street and John

Q watched the way the raindrops bounced off the brim of the deputy's hat.

'Kid,' Peyton said, 'you might be from Texas and it might be they do things different out there, but this is Light Horse County and if you want to be doubled up on a bicycle best you don't be doubled up with a negro.' With a loose smile he glanced at his partner. 'Now, I don't want to be hearing any more of that mouth you hear, not unless you want a taste of Billy.' He laid a hand across the grips of his night stick. 'Do you-all understand me?'

'Yes sir.' John Q could smell the tobacco chew on his breath.

'I swear you made a real bad start here in Georgia but you-all behave from here on out and we might just forgive you.' Peyton stood straighter then and looked the length of his nose at him. 'What're you doing this far east anyway?'

'Came to paint my grandma's house,' John Q told him, 'on account of my daddy asked me: should be done by the end of summer.'

The two men looked him up and down for a moment longer before they turned again for their car. Watching them cross the rain soaked street John Q could not stop himself from calling out. 'You know what,' he said. 'Couple of years from now I figure I'm going to be a cop myself, Texas Ranger probably like my godfather.'

'Is that a fact?' Chase had the driver's door open.

'Yes sir. Might-could be you heard of him; Frank Hamer out of San Saba County? He's the one took down Bonnie and Clyde and he's always been real fond of me.'

Pedalling off around the corner he found Pious in the shadows waiting for him. 'What the hell did you tell them that for?' he demanded.

'Tell them what?' John Q peered through the blanket of rain.

'That what you said about your godfather.'

'You know who he is?'

'If he's some kind of famous cop then they sure will and I guess that's why you told them.'

Puzzled now, John Q studied him. 'Yeah,' he said. 'That's why I told them.'

'Stupid sumbuck; don't you think it's going to piss them off?'

'Probably it will. But I said it on account of there ain't nothing my godfather hates more than cops like that throwing their weight around for no good reason.'

'Well that's just fine,' Pious said. 'But you don't got to live here do you. You don't got to live here and the last time I looked I didn't see how you was black.' Hands thrust in his pockets now, he started across the street.

John Q stared after him. He was smarting more now than when the deputy had hit him.

'Look, I'm sorry,' he said but Pious carried on up the street and John Q followed him. 'Pious, I said I'm sorry.'

'That pistol whipping they was talking about,' Pious said. 'You think that was just a whole lot of talk?'

'No, of course not....'

'I told you how they used to take it to my daddy.'

'Yeah you did.' John Q rested a hand on his shoulder. 'Bud, I'm sorry, all right? But they're gone already. You pedal from here on out.'

They rode the rest of the way across town and there was no sign of the prowl car anywhere. When they reached Spanish Bluff Pious took them the length of the driveway with John Q sitting on the handlebars. Pulling up at the garage doors, he got off and Pious leaned the bicycle against the wall. He suggested John Q stay put while he went over to the house to see if he could find Willow. Moments later he came scuttling across the patio again and a few minutes after that Willow came out from the kitchen.

Still the rain tumbled, but where there had been no wind all day it had started blowing now. Eunice opened the door upstairs and called down to her brother about how it was going to storm and she was frightened of the thunder. Pious told her there wasn't any thunder, but she said there would be soon and she did not want to be on her own. Standing there in the garage with the doors open the three of them watched the lights burning in the study on the other side of the swimming pool.

Eunice was still up there and she called down again so finally, Pious went up to talk to her.

Willow stared at John Q through the rain. 'He's had a stroke,' she said, 'my great-grandpa. He's had a stroke and he was trying to talk to me only he can't talk because that's what a stroke does to you.'

'That's what Pious said.' A little self-conscious now, John Q moved closer to her. 'What could he be trying to tell you?'

She hunched her shoulders. 'I don't know. But it was in his eyes and I know it was something important.' She pointed towards the house. 'I'm going to have to try and get in there and see him, see if he can indicate, you know, gesture maybe. It was in his eyes though, something important he wanted to tell me.'

John Q was quiet, not knowing quite what to say to her. He was not sure that trying to get into the study was a good idea though, seeing as how Morgan J had kicked everybody out. They really needed to talk to her mother but he could see no sign of the convertible.

'Where's your mother at?' he asked her.

'She's gone to the hospital in Rutherford to get some medicine.' Willow bit her lip. She looked into the rain. 'I'm scared,' she said, 'right now I'm frightened, John Q and I don't know why exactly.'

John Q worked his weight from one foot to the other. This was the first time he had been alone with her and he was feeling awkward enough that he wished Pious would hurry up and get done with his sister.

'It'll be all right.' It was all he could think of to tell her.

'What will?' Willow peered at him through the darkness.

'Everything; your great-grandpa and all, it will be okay.'

She did not say anything. She did not look as if she believed him. She just stood there with her head down and John Q wasn't sure if it had been the right thing to say or not. He couldn't think of anything else though. He looked up at the landing again, but there was still no sign of Pious.

'Okay, so listen,' he mumbled. 'I ain't sure it's the best idea you going into his study but I guess you figure you have to. But you got to wait till the coast's clear and Morgan J goes out or something.' He sniffed at the rain and he could scent a little salt in it and he figured Eunice was right and it probably was going to storm. 'Meantime,' he went on, giving himself time to think, 'there ain't no sense hovering around in the garage so why don't we go on up to the apartment?'

Willow furrowed her brow. 'What's the point of that?'

'Well.....' he said.

She was dragging at the gravel with the toe of her pump. 'I don't want to do that,' she said. 'I don't want to hide out anywhere, what's the point? I don't want Morgan J to think there's anything wrong and if he can't find me that's exactly what he will think.' She looked beyond the car once more. 'He doesn't know that I heard him and my great-grandpa talking or at least I don't think he does. So right now he can't suspect I know anything. Anyway, I'm not waiting for him to go out. What if he doesn't go anywhere?' She stepped back into the rain. 'You stay here and keep out of sight. I'll go back to my room and wait till he comes out of grandpa's study. When he does I'll come out to the balcony so you'll know and you can keep watch for him while I'm in the study.'

John Q looked on as she hurried back to the house and he was still not convinced she should be doing it because with the old man not being able to talk then what could she possibly gain? He wondered what Morgan J would do if he caught her snooping around like that and he considered the French windows that opened onto the patio. He glanced at the steps that led upstairs but there was still no sign of Pious and then another idea occurred to him. If he could get close to those French doors he might be able to see through the crack and get a look at what Morgan J was doing. He might be able to see something that would help Willow. Keeping to the shadows he made his way beyond the pool and crept under the balcony.

Pressing his eye to the crack between the doors his heart sank as he realized he couldn't actually see anything. The calico drapes were in the way and all he could make out was the white of the billowing material. He could hear a voice though; somebody was talking so he put his ear to the crack instead. It took a moment to sort of focus on what was going on and it sounded like a one way conversation. He figured that either Morgan J was talking to his father who couldn't talk back or he was talking on the phone.

————

TWELVE

Morgan J was on the phone. 'I tell you I can't find it, Chase,' he said, 'if it's here in this room he's got it so well hidden I can't lay my hands on it and I can't get him to tell me where it is on account of he can't talk.' He looked across to where his father was lying with his gaze fixed.

'He can hear I guess, but he can't talk and the way he is right now I don't suppose he'll ever talk again. I don't suppose he's got long to live now either and you ought to see the look he's giving me.' Raising the glass to his lips he sipped bourbon. 'I told him I had Shoofly all over me, but you think he'd listen to that? No sir, he doesn't give a damn about a man like Shoofly but then he doesn't know who Shoofly is.

'Do you, Dad,' he called over to the bed, 'Shoofly, he's a gangster out of Atlantic City.' Again he spoke to Chase. 'If that sonofabitch shows up down here you can handle him, right? I'm counting on you and Peyton. Told me I had seven days but I know him and he isn't going to wait that long. Give him twenty-four hours and I swear he'll be down here with a couple of his boys just looking to put the hurt on me.'

'Morgan J,' Chase said, 'let me tell you, sir, if some jigaboo out of Jersey wants to come down here not knowing his place there's a bunch of us be happy to remind him.'

Outside on the patio John Q did not hear what Chase said but he did hear Morgan Junior. He knew who he was talking to all right; he had just seen him down by the square. A sudden noise by the garage made him start, and, looking back, he spotted Pious at the foot of the steps. Very deliberately he lifted a finger to his lips and gestured for him to stay put. Once again he pressed his ear to the crack in the door.

'Anyways,' he heard Morgan J say, 'I've turned this place upside down and it's not here so have Noble get on with what you told him.'

John Q crept back across the patio. 'Morgan J is in the study,' he said to Pious, 'heard him on the phone just now talking to Chase Landry. You told me you saw them at the lunch counter right? Well, Chase's brother, that fella Noble over at the railroad you pointed out, they got him fixing to do something. Pious,' he said, 'I reckon we need to know what that something is. Willow's yonder in her bedroom right now waiting to signal when Morgan J gets done with her great-grandpa so she can go see if she can figure out what it is he wants to tell her. When she does that keep a lookout, will you?'

Pious had his mouth turned down at the corners. 'She's going in there then, is she,' he said. 'Maybe I ought to go over and tell her how it ain't such a good idea.'

John Q thought about that. 'You could try,' he said. 'But she's set on doing it anyway. Bud, when she's done have her stay put will you, at least till I get back. Her momma ain't here right now and it ain't smart for any of us to try and deal with Morgan Junior without her mom knowing what's happening.'

Pious nodded. 'Okay, I'll tell her. What-all are you going to do?'

John Q indicated where the bicycle still rested against the garage wall. 'Going to ride back to town and check out what's going on with Noble Landry.'

————

Noble had already finished most of the whiskey. Sitting inside the railroad car it was muggy, and all he could hear was the weight of the rain on the roof and the drip-drip-drip where it leaked. He was sprawled on the dusty seat with his feet crossed at the ankle on the table like he was riding first class. Only the car wasn't moving and he wasn't riding anywhere. He was drinking and thinking about working those fishing lines tomorrow and with a hangover too most probably. He was thinking about what Chase had said and how he didn't like Chase a whole lot and how he had been down on him pretty much since he had gotten home from the war in Europe.

Noble wasn't stupid: after what his brother had told him earlier he had looked at it all the way around. Nobody knew about their conversation and that's just how Chase liked to keep it. He was using the money he'd loaned him for the boat as a lever to get him to do it and as usual he wasn't paying much. Noble figured he knew where the money would be coming from though, and he figured Chase would be taking a pretty good slice of it. What they were asking he could do of course, although having only just finished one spell in the workhouse he was reluctant to risk going back for another. Besides, if he got caught it wouldn't be the workhouse this time so much as the big house and he figured that a risk like that demanded a lot more money than Chase was offering.

He told himself he would rather not do this at all. He would rather set here drinking the rest of this corn mash and hit the water again in the morning. Only there was likely to be a storm tonight and come tomorrow all the catfish would be deep in the river bed. He had to think about it some more, had to get his head all the way around it and quickly because there was the prowl car again outside. Lifting the Mason jar to his lips one more time he drank and wiped his mouth and screwed the lid back on. Searching his pocket for his tobacco sack, he took papers and made a smoke. Then he went outside.

They were both out there, Chase and Peyton riding up front in that prowl car. It was his brother who got out, engine idling where he'd pulled up just ahead of the lot.

'What say, Noble,' he called. 'You-all know what you got to do?'

'You want to get her done then, do you,' Noble muttered. 'That the way she's fallen?'

'Yes sir, that's the way she's fallen.'

Noble looked at the sky. 'Early yet, Chase: I'll get her done maybe but not right now.'

'Sure right now. I want those papers, Noble.' Chase gestured across town. 'Ain't nobody going be walking around tonight the town's going to be deserted. Give it an hour and she's going to storm so if you don't want me and Peyton beating up on you, best you-all get to it.'

———

John Q cycled back from Spanish Bluff and he could not remember doing this much pedalling in his life. In Texas he had ridden a bicycle when he was a little kid but living close to the Culpepper Ranch, he worked there weekends and for years now he'd had his own horse. He and Billy Culpepper did chores for Billy's dad and he helped with training the stock. In exchange the rancher had given him his own pony to ride, an Appaloosa filly called Rainbow that had come out of Idaho originally. Mr Culpepper told him the breed had been favored by the Nez Perce Indians and that Nez Perce was French for "pierced nose". But when John Q saw pictures of those Indians he couldn't find any of them with a hole in their nose, but he liked the horse well enough just the same. Strawberry colored and freckled across her hindquarters she was as surefooted as she was strong. It was from the back of that filly he learned how to use a catch rope and how to bring down a steer. It was how he learned about cutting horses and that's how he'd gotten the job he was to go to in the fall.

Right now though, he was on this bicycle and he pedalled into town. When he came to the indoor market he pulled off the road and around the corner as he saw that same prowl car from before. It was coming his way up the street, the two deputies inside and he thought about the phone call he had overheard just now. He watched as the car went all around the square and turned in at the sheriff's office. Only when the deputies were inside the building did he come out of the shadows and cycle on.

Finally he came to the raised cinder causeway where the railroad ran and he picked out the wrecked automobiles and railroad cars. There was light in the fancy one with the faded paint and gold lettering on the side. Stowing the bicycle in some bushes, he carried on afoot. Tentative now, he was cautious; keeping to the shadows he had not bothered to put on a slicker because that was bright yellow and would give him away. The rain wasn't cold. It was just wet and there was lots of it and he was soaked to the skin by the time he made it the length of the Barra driveway. Now his clothes stuck to him, shirt and jeans, the rain was inside his boots and his feet squelched with every step. He didn't care. He was thinking about Willow and how she had been earlier, how she told him that she was frightened but couldn't say exactly why.

Taking cover in the lee of one of the wrecked automobiles he scanned the empty lot and tried to figure out what he was doing there and what he might discover. He was trying to work out what his godfather would do in a situation like this and decided it would be surveillance first most probably.

———

Noble was watching him with a smile on his face. He had spotted him stow the bicycle in those bushes from where he stood smoking his cigarette at the door of the Pullman. He watched as he moved stealthily across to that old Chevy where it lay on its side. That kid wasn't nearly stealthy enough and even by this light Noble thought he knew who it was. He had seen him on the cinder rise with Pious Noon yesterday and again on the river this morning.

Leaning in the doorway he supped a little more of the corn mash then re fixed the lid on the jar. Finishing his cigarette, he fetched his daddy's oilskin coat his mother had given him after the old man passed away. He used to fish The Dividing rather than the river and wore one of the old style coats the trawlermen had only in olive green instead of the yellow they favored today. Slipping the coat around his shoulders Noble went out into the rain where the wind was up and by the weight of salt in the air, he knew it was going to storm and storm badly.

Squinting across the lot he could make out that denser shadow by the automobile where the kid was still hiding and he considered walking over there and hauling him out by his ear. But the fact the kid was there at all intrigued him and he wouldn't put it past his brother to pay somebody to make sure he did what he'd been told. Chase was like that; sumbuck would double-cross you if he could and he covered every angle. If Noble stopped to think about it he could probably find his brother's hand in most of the appearances he'd made at the county courthouse.

———

John Q tailed him all the way across town. He kept well back, the same side of the street only moving when Noble moved and stopping when Noble paused. He followed him as far as the square then along the sidewalk beyond the drugstore and the cash grocery onto Maple Street. They were coming into the business district now and that meant no more stores but warehouses, fruit sellers; cotton and tobacco. There were offices down this way and the lot behind the train station where the city parked its buses.

A few blocks further the street opened into small lots with grassy yards and individual buildings. Noble paused outside one that was set well back from the road. White Clapboard, it was not very big; an old house, maybe a couple of rooms but no more. The backyard was separated from the front by a fence and it looked to John Q like this place had been somebody's home when it was built but wasn't used as a home anymore. There was a sign out front and with the way the wind was blowing it was swinging back and forth.

For a long time Noble studied it. For a long time he stood there stiffly. His shoulders set under that long coat he seemed rooted almost for a while. John Q remained a block back, hovering in the shadow of two oak trees, his clothes so wet they felt like a second skin.

Noble moved off finally, John Q watching as he crossed the lawn heading toward the fence at the back where he disappeared from view. Keeping low, John Q followed as far as he dare but there was no cover here and he did not want to be caught out in the open. He could read the sign however from out on the sidewalk: "Mortimer & Rayburn - Attorneys at Law".

———

THIRTEEN

Back at Spanish Bluff, Morgan J came out of his father's study and closed the door. No sooner had he done that than Mama Sox appeared from the kitchen wiping her hands on her apron. 'Is everything all right, Mr Morgan?'

For a moment he just looked at her with his lip wrinkled and his eyebrow raised. 'No, Mama, everything is not all right. What kind of a question is that? How could everything be all right? You saw the doctor. You saw my father. He's had a stroke. Don't you understand what that means?' His tone was terse, vicious almost. From the landing where Willow was hovering, she flinched at every word.

Mama Sox stood where she was, hands still caught in her apron. Peeking over the banister, Willow could see tears in her eyes.

'My father is dying,' Morgan J told her. 'He's not getting any better. He's only going to get worse, don't you understand that?'

A little dumbly Mama nodded.

'When he's gone this will be my house and things are going to change so don't get comfortable above the garage there because I aim to sell up and there's no guarantee that you'll be staying on as housekeeper.'

He started up the stairs and Willow scuttled back to her room. She heard him pause, his weight causing the boards to creak on the partially carpeted stairs.

'Is Mrs Flood here?' he called. 'Mama Sox, is Mrs Flood in her room?'

'No sir, she done gone to Rutherford.'

'I thought she just came from there.'

'She done that sure: but the doctor don't got what-all he needs with the medicine. Mrs Flood went back to Rutherford because it's only at the hospital they got what Mr Barra has to have so the doctor wrote up a prescription.'

Willow watched through the crack in the door, Morgan J still on the stairs with one hand on the banister rail. 'Mrs Flood is driving her car?'

'Yes sir, she is.'

'It's going to storm, Mama,' he uttered the words slowly, ominously, a weight to them. 'I heard it on the radio just now, a big storm all along the coast. She shouldn't be driving, not on these roads, not in this weather. Who knows what could happen.'

Watching him Willow was trembling. Those words; the sinister way he was talking, it was more than just words. She watched him continue up the stairs then pause when he got to the landing.

'Mama Sox,' he called down a second time and Willow heard the housekeeper again in the hall.

'Yes sir?'

'Where's Willow?'

She froze; the tone of his voice, the questions about her mother. Moving quickly now she crossed the room and stepped onto the balcony where she closed the glass door. She was only just in time because the door from the landing opened and she could see him, heavy set, his face flushed red from all his drinking. He had deep set eyes and they sought her out tracing the room this way and that to see if she was there. He did not call out. He just stood where he was in the doorway and for a long time he stared at the balcony.

Willow was crouched to the side of the glass door with the iron fili-gree of the rail gripped between her fingers. She shot a glance across the pool to where a shadow lurked in the lee of the garage. She was expecting John Q but it was Pious she saw. For a moment she did not know what to do. Then she made her way along the balcony to the corner where a pillar supported the weight from below. Climbing over the rail she slid down the pillar to the ground as she had done countless times before.

Quickly she crossed the patio.

'Miss Willow,' Pious moved out from the shadows, 'what's going on?'

'Morgan J just came out of the study.' Willow indicated the house. 'He's upstairs right now looking for me but I'm going to go back and see if I can talk to my great-grandpa.'

Pious stared at her. 'You sure you want to be doing that, I mean if Morgan J is looking for you?'

'He's upstairs.' Again she pointed. 'Look, you can see there, that's his light in the bedroom. Pious,' she said. 'What happened to John Q?'

'Gone into town; said to me how I had to keep watch for you.' He gestured. 'Took my bicycle on account of he heard Mr Morgan talking on the phone. Something to do with cops, Miss Willow, something to do with Noble Landry.'

———

John Q was on his way back to the railroad car. With Noble having gone around back of that attorney's office he figured he must be attempting to break in. It was not as if he could go to the cops or anything though, because it seemed to be cops that were behind this. There was no point hanging around until Noble came out again so he decided to go back to the Pullman. It occurred to him that the car would be empty right now and there might be something inside that would give him a clue as to what was happening.

He made his way across town again as quickly as he could and with so much rain having fallen, the muddy sidewalk was already giving way. It made the going difficult, but he got there slipping and sliding and on the edge of the open lot he paused where a light burned in the railroad car. The ground here was mush and the boots he was wearing had slope heels and gave no grip. He was stumbling, trying to keep his balance but so much water had settled little rivers trailed all across the lot. It was a dump; he had seen that from the cinder rise, holes in the ground and bits and pieces of old automobile, bits of railroad car. In the darkness he could not see them and he had to pick his way very carefully. That was not easy though, with the ground as slippery as it was. He had just about made it to the Pullman when he thought he heard a noise behind him. Heart in his mouth he whirled around, put his foot in a hole and went down so hard he remembered nothing after.

——

Back at Spanish Bluff, Pious watched Willow cross beyond the swimming pool to the French windows that led to Mr Barra's study. His job was to keep watch for Morgan J and from where he was right now he could not do it properly.

Upstairs in the apartment he switched off the light then took up position at the kitchen window. He could see the main house where all the lights were burning. He could see the window that Willow said was Morgan Junior's and he could see his shadow moving back and forth.

His sister came through from the room she shared with their mama. 'Pious,' she said, 'why you switched all the lights off?'

'Can see better in the dark.'

'See what better?' She came and stood next to him.

He pointed. 'You see that window yonder over on the balcony?'

'Uh-huh.'

'I want you to watch with me, see what-all shadows you can make out, you know like of a person moving.'

'What for?'

'Just a game I'm playing with Miss Willow. Mr Morgan is supposed to be in his room and we need to know if he leaves out. You want to watch with me, Eunice, don't you?'

'Sure. I want to watch with you.'

'All right,' he looked sideways at her now. 'You see anything I don't, make sure you holler okay?'

——

Taking care to be as quiet as she could, Willow slipped inside her great-grandpa's study. Morgan J's bedroom was directly overhead and she could hear him pacing the wooden floor. She told herself that as long as she could hear him she knew where he was and could risk being there.

Quietly, she approached the bed. The single lamp seemed very dim and it was all that illuminated the room. The old man lay on his back with his mouth open and his eyes closed, he was breathing very lightly. Willow noticed how his eyelids were fluttering but he was not asleep, he was awake and he must have heard her because he opened his eyes and half-turning his head, he looked directly at her. It seemed such an effort. All he could manage was to twist his neck muscles just so far. His eyes were milky, clouded across the pupil. Spittle traced a line on his lip and Willow used a tissue from the box the nurse had left to wipe it away.

He could not talk, he could not utter a sound; he just lay there looking at her with his right hand loose of the bedclothes and still curled up in a fist. Gently Willow laid a hand across that fist and his skin seemed so chill it was as if there was no blood in him.

'Grandpa,' she said. 'Can you understand me?'

He blinked once, slowly; and the movement seemed deliberate. Willow wasn't sure but perhaps that was his way of responding.

'Does that blink mean yes?' she asked him.

He closed his eyes once more.

'You wanted to see me. I know you wanted to talk to me,' she was whispering, conscious of the footsteps above her head. 'When the nurse was here with the doctor I tried to come in and see you, but she wouldn't let me. Grandpa, I know you wanted to talk to me.'

She could feel his hand tremble where she held it. Again he blinked and another line of spittle was loosed and again she wiped it away. 'What did you want to say to me?' she asked. 'Can you show me?'

His eyes seemed to glass with tears, anger maybe; frustration, the need to speak, his mind alert but not able to put his thoughts into words. He managed to open his mouth a fraction.

'What is it, Grandpa?' Willow clutched his hand more tightly. 'Was it about Morgan J? I heard the two of you talking. This morning when I was up on the balcony I heard you talking, Grandpa. I heard what you said to Morgan J.'

He stared at her now, either fear in his eyes or was it hope maybe. She could not tell. He could move his eyes and he worked them sideways and Willow looked where he indicated; the desk, the chair set before it, the book cases fixed to the wall.

'What is it?' she asked him. 'Are you trying to show me where something is? Is it the desk, Grandpa? What am I looking for?'

Letting go of his hand she crossed to the oak desk with the inset leather blotter and cushioned swivel chair. Papers lay strewn across the top, muddled and disorderly and that was not like her great-grandpa at all. She realised that Morgan J must have been rooting through the desk when he had been down here earlier.

When she turned again the old man was watching her. He seemed to be straining, had managed to twist his head a little more and he was looking beyond her across the desk to the bookshelves that lined the far wall.

'Is it a book?' she asked him. 'Is it somewhere on those bookshelves?'

Straining even more now she could see a vein pulse in his forehead.

'The desk maybe,' she suggested. 'Is it in the desk?' She was looking for him to blink again but his gaze seemed to falter, eyelids fluttering as if the effort was too much and she went back to the bed.

'You'll be all right, Grandpa,' she assured him. 'Everything will be all right, you'll get better. I know you will.'

The muscles in his face sagged now, his cheeks hollow; his mouth was slack, lips forming an oval against his teeth. His eyes closed and they remained that way as if he couldn't keep them open any longer. Willow held his hand and then she realised that she could no longer hear Morgan J. Her blood ran cold as she heard him on the stairs suddenly. Seconds later he was in the hall and crossing to the study.

Panic took her.

No time to get to the patio.

No time to make her escape.

Her great-grandpa's eyes were open again and her own fear seemed echoed in his pupils. Letting go his hand Willow dropped to the floor and scuttled under the bed. She was barely out of sight when the door opened and light flooded the study from the hall. She heard the door close and Morgan J's footsteps sounded on the wooden boards. Willow could see his shoes, black and polished; she could pick out the laces, the turn-ups on the legs of his pants.

He stood there by the bed but he did not say anything. The only thing Willow could hear was the sound of her breathing and the thump of her heart in her chest and she was sure he could hear it too. At any moment he would drop to one knee, reach under the bed and drag her out by her hair. But he didn't. He could not have heard her because he spoke now, his voice deep; it seemed to resonate in the confines of the room.

'Old man,' he said. 'I swear I looked everywhere and I can't find those papers and I have to tell you, you really shouldn't have hidden them. All it does is string this out and it isn't going to do any good. Do you hear me? It isn't going to do any good.'

Of course his father could not respond and Morgan J sat down heavily in the chair. Willow could see his legs where they were crossed at the knee. She could see the top of his socks where his pants rode up. She could see pale flesh and black hairs and she stared at one foot as it swung back and forth.

'On account of it I had to get wheels in motion elsewhere,' Morgan J told him. 'Do you understand what I'm talking about? You won't tell me where the paperwork is at so I figured Mortimer would probably know and right about now I got people paying his place a visit.' He sat forward then, both feet on the floor. 'Understand this now, won't you: either those papers burn or they do. It doesn't much matter which it is because with the weather this bad, accidents always happen. You know Cassie's in her automobile right now, don't you? Oh yes, she's headed for Rutherford to get your medicine. I tell you, with the way this storm's blowing there'll be trees down and power lines, it sure as hell isn't any time to be on the road.'

Under the bed it was all Willow could do not to cry out. She had her hand to her mouth, fingers pasted over her lips. Above her she felt her great-grandpa try and move but he was so frail, so light, there was barely a murmur in the bedsprings at all.

'Don't think I won't do it,' Morgan J went on. 'I got people swarming all over me right now and they are not the kind to hold off just because my name is Barra. I told you how it was; I got debts sold on in Atlantic City and to Shoofly of all people. That's one black sonofabitch doesn't know his place and he isn't scared of taking down a white man. I think it's why Dandy Nicholls sold to him. I think Dandy got a kick out of it. It could've been avoided though, if you'd let me develop the island back when I wanted I wouldn't be in this fix right now.'

He got to his feet, shoving back the chair so forcefully it scraped on the boards and from where she lay Willow could see lines in the polished floor.

'It's me or them, old man; the paperwork or that squatter you adopted and her brat of a daughter.' Morgan J stooped now, his head close to the bed. Willow could see the heels of his shoes off the floor. 'You better pray old Mortimer hasn't made it too hard to find those papers because one way or another I'm going to have what's coming to me.'

———

FOURTEEN

John Q opened his eyes but the gloom did not seem to dissipate at all. His eyes hurt. His head hurt, the whole right side of his face seemed to pulse with pain. Gingerly he lifted a hand, touched fingers to his temple and they came away sticky. Blood, dried pretty much already, but blood all the same.

'Leave that be now,' a voice told him. 'I just got done there fixing to it.'

John Q didn't recognise the voice. He tried to see who it was talking to him but he could not make them out because in this light his vision was blurred.

'Best you lay where you're at,' the voice suggested; 'found you lying out there with a pretty good lunk on the noggin and I don't know who you are or what you think you're doing but best you lay where you be.'

John Q did just that. He did not think he could move anyway, his limbs were like lead and his back stiff, he lay where he was on some kind of mattress that was thin and vague and felt as if it were filled with chicken wire. The place smelled of kerosene and engine oil and that made him think about Pious and from Pious his thoughts turned to Willow and her great-grandpa's study.

He could smell something other than oil; kind of musty, like damp maybe. It had been raining all day and he tried to hear if it was raining still. He had closed his eyes to the pain, but he opened them again now and slowly things began to slip into focus.

The ceiling was sort of domed and narrow and it seemed to be a long way above him. He was lying on his back and he could see the figure of a man hunched over him. He felt a cool sensation against his forehead as a damp cloth was pressed to his eye. John Q tried to speak but his mouth had dried out and his tongue felt so thick he could not summon a single word.

'You-all need a drink of water?' the voice came at him again then the man moved off and John Q thought he heard the sound of some kind of dipper being pitched into a barrel. Moments later the man was back and he lifted his head and held the dipper so he could sip the water.

The man came more into focus and John Q had no idea who he was, but the way that ceiling was shaped and how it was so narrow he realised he was in a railroad car and then it all came back to him. The ground so slippery outside; with the sudden noise he had spun round, stepped in a hole and got knocked out with the fall.

'Took a pretty good whack yes you did,' Noble Landry, it was as if he could guess what John Q was thinking, 'found you right by the door.' He sat back on one leg, his other knee drawn up to his chin and John Q could smell the sickly scent of corn mash on his breath now. Beyond him he could see the back of one of the Pullman's seats with dust half an inch thick across it. The seat formed a barrier between where the mattress was laid out and the rest of the car as if this space was Noble's bedroom. It occurred to him that it was Noble's bedroom.

Raising himself up on one elbow, he took the dipper Noble still held and drank the rest of the water. Noble was peering at him. Getting to his feet he moved to the arm of the seat and worked strings of tobacco from the sack he carried in the bib pocket of his overalls. John Q could smell something else now and he figured it was fish guts and he recalled how he and Pious had seen Noble in a rowboat on the river this morning.

Noble built his cigarette, rolled it; then carefully he snaked his tongue along the strip of gum on the paper. Striking a match he flapped it out and drew deeply, blew smoke then turning the cigarette out-wise he offered it to John Q.

'I been known to,' John Q shook his head, 'but my momma ain't happy about it and right now I'm sick to my stomach and I reckon it's all I can do to hang on to the water you-all brung me.'

Noble chuckled. 'Can get you like that a knock on the head.' His eyes dulled slightly. 'Kid,' he said. 'I knowed you was right behind me all the way from when I stepped out of this here Pullman. Saw you from the doorway where you were crouched back there thinking you was out of sight, so you better tell me what were you doing tailing me?'

For a long time John Q stared at him. He did not answer and he was afraid now suddenly.

'Was it Chase had you follow me?'

John Q just looked at him.

'Was it? Wouldn't put anything past that sumbuck and he's supposed to be family.' Noble worked the ashes from the end of his cigarette. 'Who-all told you to follow me?'

'I wasn't following you.' It was all John Q could think of to say.

'You were just strolling around in a rain storm then were you,' Noble leered at him, 'just hanging out with all this rain coming down and the wind blowing like she is. Don't lie to me, kid,' he said. 'I hate liars about as bad as I hate anybody: ain't nothing in this world worse than a liar because you can't trust nothing if you can't trust that what's said.' He cocked his head to one side. 'I've seen you around, seen you up on the rise with Mama Sox's boy and I seen you on the river. So come on now who are you?'

'I'm John Q, Grandma Quarrie's grandson. She lives on Riverview Road.'

'Grandma Quarrie?' Noble cocked one eyebrow: 'You telling me you're kin to Grandma Q used to be the midwife around these parts? Well, I'll be damned, she's the one brung me into this world along with I figure most everybody.' Drawing hard on his cigarette his tone was a little gentler. 'Kid,' he said, 'you were following me acrost town and you still ain't told me why. Come on now, spit it out and make sure it's the truth you hear me?'

Heart thumping, John Q took a breath. 'All right,' he said. 'I was following you but nobody told me to do it. I know your brother is a cop, Noble and he was on the phone. It was Morgan Barra Junior talking to him and I was over here on account of that.'

Noble peered at him. 'What does a kid like you know about Morgan Barra Junior?'

'I know he's real worried about something right now and I figure it's on account of a girl named Willow Flood likes to buy soda from the drugstore come Saturday.'

'Willow Flood,' Noble flicked ash. 'So you know that little peach, do you? Sweet on her some then are you?'

John Q felt color bruise his cheekbones.

'She's a cutie,' Noble went on, 'going to be even cuter. Don't tell me you ain't noticed.'

'I ain't noticed,' John Q told him. 'And I ain't sweet on anybody. Listen, Noble. I'm out of San Saba County, Texas and my godfather is Frank Hamer. You ever hear of him?'

Noble did not say whether he had or not but he did fall silent. John Q tried to get up but his head swam and Noble told him to stay where he was. 'Right now there ain't any getting up for you,' he said, 'even if I had a mind to let you.'

Outside they heard the sound of a car approaching and moments later the beam from a set of headlights swept the grimy window. Nostril's flared Noble reached to the table for a yellow envelope and stuffed it inside his overalls.

'You want to stay alive,' he said, 'best you lie where you're at and pull that blanket clear over your head. Make it look like there ain't nobody back there.' He indicated the soiled blanket lying on the floor next to the mattress. 'Right now we got the kind of company that finds you here you'll wish you'd never got quit of that bicycle.'

———

Willow led the way up the garden; the wind cutting across the open ground and the rain falling at a vicious slant. She was wearing an oilskin and Pious trotted behind her having thrown the cape Albert had given him around his shoulders. He kept looking back towards the house. Willow hadn't told him what had happened, but when she crossed the driveway to the garage just now she had no color in her cheeks at all.

Keeping to the shadows cast by the oak trees they picked their way to where a series of wooden steps shouldered the height of the bluff. They led down to the mooring and normally the water down there was languid, drifting along at nothing more than a meander. But it wasn't like that now. Now there was a real chop to it; angry looking white-capped waves; even from the bluff they could see the way the swell was sweeping upriver.

The wooden steps carried a steep angle and they were slick and oily with rain. Taking them very carefully, they made the jetty where Willow's little skiff was pinched between two larger boats that belonged to her great-grandfather. All three were rippling uneasily.

'Miss Willow,' Pious had to raise his voice above the howl of the wind. 'Listen to me; you can't be crossing the shoals in weather like this.'

'I have to, Pious. I have to get away from here and the island is the only place I'll be safe.'

He was shaking his head. 'I'm telling you; go out in that bay tonight and you won't have to worry about being safe, you won't have to worry about nothing. That wind will have you out of that boat so fast you'll be but a couple of bites for them bull sharks. We need to figure something else here so why don't you go ahead and tell me what happened in your great-grandpa's study?'

Willow considered him then for a moment. She considered the skiff tied stern and bow, the way the ropes were straining at the cleats on the jetty. She bit her lip and before she realised it, tears were rolling down her cheeks.

'He's going to kill me,' she cried. 'Morgan J is going to kill me and he's going to kill my mother too. I heard him threaten to do it. Right now he's looking for some papers, but if he can't find them he's going to burn me and my mother.' She sobbed now. 'That's what he said. He's going to burn us, Pious. I heard him tell my great-grandpa.'

Pious stared at her with his mouth hanging open. 'Burn you? He ain't going to that, Miss Willow; not Morgan J.'

'Yes he is. I heard him say it. If he can't find the papers he'll have no choice. That's what he said.' Again she looked at the cleats, the way the boat was shifting. 'It must be great-grandpa's will he's talking about. If what I heard is right then Morgan J isn't going to get any money. It's going to my mother instead and there has to be something somewhere that says so. There has to be papers and I think that's what my great-grandpa was trying to tell me. I think he wanted me to find his will so I could give it to my mother. If everybody knew what he planned to do with his money then Morgan J wouldn't be able to do anything to us because it would be too obvious.' She threw out a hand. 'But he can't tell me where it is because he can't talk and my mother went to the hospital so she has no idea any of this is happening. Pious,' she sobbed, 'what am I going to do?'

They stood in the gathering storm with the weight of the river pressing the pilings beneath them. 'Well whatever it is,' Pious told her, 'it ain't crossing to Half-Mile Island. You can't make it. I know them tides same as you do and you can't get over there tonight, not without the boat taking water.'

Willow bit her lip. 'I have to. There's nowhere else to go.'

'Sure there is,' suddenly he was smiling. 'Throw off that bowline yonder. Don't worry, Miss Willow: I know where-all I can bring you.'

———

John Q lay as if he were dead. He was wary of Noble but Chase really bothered him. He was thinking about just how badly he had messed up here and tried to excuse himself with the fact that he was up against the worst kind of people. He remembered how often his Uncle Frank had told him that the criminal is like a coyote, always pausing to throw a glance over its shoulder.

He concentrated on not moving a muscle. He recognised Chase's voice from when he had stopped him and Pious on the bicycle and he could hear his partner as well. Neither of them sounded very happy.

'What's going on, Noble?' It was Chase talking. 'We swung by the attorney's office just now and there ain't no sign of you ever having been there.'

Noble took a moment before he answered. 'Couldn't get her done,' he said. 'Couldn't get to her on account of some kid was following me. I figured you sent him, Chase, sent him to keep an eye on me.'

'Why would I do that?' Chase sounded incredulous. 'Noble, what the hell are you talking about?'

'Some kid. I told you he was following me so I couldn't get near that attorney's office.'

'Where's he at now this kid?'

'Beats me, soon as I figured he was tailing me I took off and I imagine he done too. Don't know where he got to and I don't care. Seeing him like that kind of shook me up, Chase. Made me realise that if I got caught it ain't the workhouse I'll be heading for it's the big house.'

Chase let go a breath that John Q could hear from where he lay behind the seats. 'Noble,' he said, 'you have to get down there and get those papers. You don't - what the hell do we tell Morgan J?'

'Tell him what you like,' Noble said. 'I ain't doing it; didn't want to from the get-go. I only said I would on account of how you're putting the squeeze on me.'

'You sonofabitch,' his brother said, 'that ain't what you told me when I came by here this afternoon. What's up with you, Noble that you're fretting about some pinch that ain't going to happen? Me and Peyton's the law here in case you-all forgotten.'

'Yeah well I done changed my mind,' Noble told him. 'I'm done with the kind of business you been offering. Three times in my life I been down the road on account of you, Chase and where-all has it got me?'

From where he lay John Q heard the crack of a Billy Club followed by a grunt and then the floor shuddered where he assumed Noble went down. He heard the scuffle of feet and then another grunt as somebody kicked out and he lay as still as the grave. He heard another kick then the sound of somebody breathing hard and finally a voice lifted.

'Leave him,' Peyton said, 'can't be kicking your own kin to death, Chase, that ain't natural.'

'You know something,' Chase said. 'I'm about sick of this, I swear.'

Peyton sighed. 'On account of it's been all this time already, all these years and that slice of pie we were promised way back when ain't come to diddley?'

'No kidding,' Chase said.

'You know, when I found Morgan J lying by Bluff Bridge that time he didn't know Saturday from Tuesday.'

John Q was listening intently.

'Cassie Flood wasn't but ten years old and her momma drowned and on account of what we did Morgan J stayed out of prison.'

'I hear you,' Chase echoed. 'Fact is he owes us plenty and right now it ain't you and me got some jig out of Atlantic City wanting a piece of us. Come on,' he said, 'let's get out of here. Noble wasn't ever going to be any use, should've figured that from the get-go.'

'So what-all are we going to do then?' Peyton said.

'I don't know yet. Think on her some maybe, swing by that attorney's office ourselves and see if we can't get in.'

'I ain't sure we want to be breaking into an attorney's office, Chase. All right if it's Noble doing her but anybody sees us how're we going to explain it?'

'Well I figure it's either that or we just go ahead and cut our losses.'

At that Peyton seemed to falter. 'Hold on now,' he said, 'we can't do that. Not after it's been so long. Without getting this figured out Morgan J don't got his money and we don't got what's owing.' He paused for a moment then he added. 'Didn't he sit there in Murphy's place and say how if it ain't the paperwork then we have deal with Cassie?'

'That's what he said; Peyton. You telling me you'd rather be dealing with her than busting into an attorney's office?'

'Chase, I ain't sure what I'm telling you. But whatever we do, we got to figure this out because we come too far already and I got plans for my retirement.'

When John Q heard the engine start up he threw off the blanket and witnessed the wash of headlights once more against the window. Through the thin light that still drifted from the hurricane lamp he spotted Noble picking himself up off the floor with blood leaking from a cut at his mouth. He was holding one arm across his belly but he had a smile on his face despite it.

'Hope you got all that,' he said. 'You see it just occurred to me how you being here could get me out of a tight spot maybe if it comes to it. If what I got in mind goes to rat-shit, which it probably will, I just might need you to talk to somebody because my kin will be looking for me and you can see how he feels about family.' He broke off then to catch his breath. 'Kid,' he said, 'fact is I'm going to have to truss you up for a while here to make sure you don't run off on me.'

He got to his feet. A string of blood dripped from his mouth and he wiped it. Opening the Mason jar he took a sip. Then he pulled the envelope from his bib pocket and as he did he winced at the pain in his ribs.

'You know what,' he said. 'My brother's so dumb he can't see how I got in there even though of course I did.' He looked down at John Q briefly. 'Know how to pick me a lock see, not as if I ain't done it before. Chase's problem is how it's been so long since he done any real police work he can't see when a lock's been tampered.' He sat down now and swallowed whiskey. 'The way I left it that lawyer ain't going to know nothing is missing unless he opens up his cabinet for that file and that file only.'

John Q had no idea what he was talking about.

'Need to go out for a while now and you're going to stay put. You're going lie nice and quiet because the only person likely to swing by again is my brother and you really don't want to him to find you.' He was smiling now, talking to himself. 'Going to go up the road to the hotel there and make me a phone call. Yes, sir; got me a call to make and that ought to bring in enough dough to get me quit of this place.' Again he looked at John Q. 'You stay put and I'll be letting you out of here just as soon as I get back. You don't, you try and get away now, I swear I'll be along Riverview Road with a fillet knife I might just whet on your grandma.'

———

FIFTEEN

Pious steered the boat upriver with Willow sitting in the prow. Eyes pinned against the spray he picked a path midstream where the waves kicked up pretty bad but at least the boat wasn't going to be wrecked on the shore.

'It'll be okay,' he called when Willow peered back at him through the gloom. 'Ain't no way I was going to let you cross the shoals tonight, your mama done lost her own mama, she lost her husband and I ain't about to let her lose you as well.'

'What're we going to do then?' Willow shouted. 'Where are you taking me?'

'Miss Willow, don't worry about any of it. You'll see where we're going when we get there and when I get you fixed up I'll take this boat back and tie her off and won't anybody know where you're at. I can talk to your mama when she gets home from fetching the medicine. I'll tell her what you found out, how I took you out of there and got you safe. After that she'll be able to figure out what to do about Morgan J.'

A quarter of an hour later they made the final turn to the landing and, sculling across the waves tops, Pious eased the little craft into slacker water. Tying off next to Grandma Q's boat, he offered a hand to Willow. She did not recognise the jetty or the boat and she looked at him with a puzzled expression on her face.

'Where are we, Pious?' she asked.

Pious pointed above their heads. 'Yonder's Riverview Road and that's where Grandma Q lives, the midwife what delivered your mama?'

'John Q's grandma?'

'That's right. I'm going to hide you out in the workshop back of the house till John Q gets home and the three of us can figure this out.' Taking her hand he led the way. 'Careful now, this old staircase is steep and slippery.'

They climbed the steps and when they got to the yard Pious squatted down on his haunches. The rain was falling even harder than it had been earlier and with the wind swirling through the trees the yard was a maelstrom of flying leaves. He pointed beyond the house where lights burned in the kitchen then he started across the lawn but the shadow of Grandma Q crossed the window and he crouched again pulling Willow down beside him. The shadow disappeared once more and the two of them ran at a crouch to the workshop.

It was dry inside; no leaks in the roofing tin despite the way the wind seemed to want to pull it up at the corners.

'I figure you'll know when John Q gets back,' Pious said. 'If he comes by the big house I'll tell him where you're at. His grandma likes to go to bed and take to reading a book so you-all can swing around the back no problem. John Q's room is the one they got yonder but I'll be sure and tell him you're holed up here.' He smiled now and nodded to her. 'Set tight and you'll be safe. I got to get that skiff back downriver before they figure she's gone and start wondering.'

Willow peered into his face through the shadows. 'What if John Q doesn't come back?' she asked him.

He seemed to think about that. 'Figure he's got to sometime, but if he don't you just set this storm out and by then your mom ought to be home from the hospital.'

'As soon as the weather breaks I'm going to Half-Mile Island.'

Pious clicked his tongue. 'Miss Willow that's just what he'd expect. If Morgan J really does want to kill you he's going to be looking for you over there before he looks anyplace else.'

'It doesn't matter. I can hide out: the McElroy house maybe or the McHenry ruins, you know there are tunnels down there at Fermanagh.'

His eyes widened. 'What tunnels?'

'Under the ruins of the house, they built tunnels under there that run all the way to the beach.'

Pious was not convinced. 'Miss Willow,' he said. 'That's Morgan J's island you're talking about. I figure if you-all know about tunnels then he surely does as well.'

He left her then and Willow watched the yellow bob of his oilskin as he cut across the lawn in the darkness. There was a wooden stool pressed under the bench, the kind of thing Grandma Q would stand on when she was cutting back stuff that was growing too tall maybe. Willow pulled it out and set it against the wall and she sat down to think about her mother on the road in this weather making the journey back from Rutherford.

———

Noble tied John Q with baling twine he had scavenged from the rag picker. He used plenty, securing the boy's hands behind his back and his legs at the ankle. All the while he was doing it John Q was scouring the railroad car for some sharpened object; something he could use to cut himself free again. His gaze settled on a rusting hinge where the door had been. It was at the far end of the car though, and he would have to get there. Noble finished tying his wrists and he winced at the lack of blood in his fingers.

'You sure you got her tight enough?' he said. 'You sure you don't want to tweak her a little more maybe?'

'Kid, don't be getting sassy now, don't give me no trouble here because I don't want to be putting the hurt on you. Set tight and you can get clear of this soon as I'm done with my phone call.'

Crossing to the doorway he peered out into the rain. Pressing a palm to the bib of his overalls he sniffed the air and shook his head and cursed now softly. John Q heard him muttering about ink running and everything and again he shook his head. Taking the envelope from his overalls he gave a short glance around the confines of the Pullman where the walls were still papered in places; a covering that once upon a time had been expensive but now was peeling badly. He considered a patch to the left of the window that had bagged to the point where he could slip the envelope between the covering and the wall.

'Ought to hold her,' he said and, with another quick look at his prisoner, he ducked outside.

He was gone and John Q lay there for a moment to make sure he was not hovering by the doorway still. He considered the rusty hinge. It was high enough up the jamb that he would have to get to his feet in order to reach it and he would have to think about that. First he had to get over there and the only way he could do that was to work his way on his bottom. Using the wall behind the mattress he wriggled around on his side then managed to press himself against the wall so he could shuffle upright. Backwards now he worked his heels into the floor to propel himself beyond the table and seats to the door.

It seemed to take an eternity to get there and with his hands tied like they were he was unstable and toppled over. He cracked his head so hard he almost knocked himself out again and it was just about all he could manage to work himself upright.

This was taking too long and he was sure Noble would come back anytime or Chase and Peyton maybe. If they found him he was dead and he wasn't sure he would not be that way with Noble either. The man was a mess of things there was other way to look at it. Almost friendly at times and yet what he had said about a fillet knife and John Q's grandma, it occurred to him Noble might actually be one of those psychopaths his Uncle Frank talked about; the kind of man who was just as at home in the nuthouse as he was the jailhouse.

He had to keep going and once again he worked his way backwards. It took a few more minutes but he got across the floor and shuffled himself around so his back was to the doorway where that hinge protruded coated with rust but set fast. He had to get to his feet and that was not going to be easy with the way his ankles were locked together and that baling twine was cutting off the circulation. He took a moment to catch his breath with rain water blowing across him.

It took a while but he persevered, rocking back and forth on his ankles and using the wall again to support him. He got his feet flat on the floor so they could take his weight then he used the doorjamb at his back as a pivot and that way he wriggled upright. Now he was standing and he could feel the hinge where it stuck out cold and sharp at his spine. He figured it had enough of an edge to it and with a good view of the road still, he began to saw his wrists up and down.

———

Pious made it back to the jetty at Spanish Bluff. Securing the boat between Mr Barra's two big launches he headed up the steps with the wind dragging at his clothes. Momentarily the rain seemed to have eased but the wind howled in his ears all the way from the landing to the top of the steps where the path spilled into the garden.

The house was a good distance from where the path came out; set back beyond the lawn and the pool and patio. There was nobody outside right now and he could see lights above the garage where his sister would be worrying about the storm. He could see lights in the kitchen where his mama was working and lights in the bedrooms upstairs. He crept down the side of the lawn keeping to the beds of turned earth where Mr Barra's roses grew. He kept to the deepest shadows because the closer he got the further the lights cast and he did not want to be answering any questions.

Finally he was so close he could smell cigar smoke and there was only one person who smoked cigars in this house. He stopped moving. Now he remained very still. From the shadows he could pick out Morgan J standing at the glass doors that led to his father's study. He was half out on the patio and half in the study as if he hadn't been sure whether he wanted to come outside after all. He seemed to be staring directly across the swimming pool though, and straight at Pious. Crouched there Pious did not move a muscle. It looked for all-the-world as if Morgan J was staring at him and he wondered if he hadn't seen him and Willow when they snuck down to the landing.

The grass damp under his feet he had one hand pressed to the flower beds so he could support his weight and that yellow oilskin was bound to give him away. On the other side of the patio Morgan J smoked his cigar and Pious thought he heard the telephone ringing. His mama would answer it and he switched his gaze from the study doors to the kitchen window and saw her wipe her hands on a towel.

Still Morgan J stood where he was only now he had his head cocked like a dog. Chin high, he seemed to be listening and then he stepped back inside the study and closed the doors.

Taking his chance Pious skipped across the garden to the driveway where the garage stood open. Albert was in the little workshop at the back and he looked up as the boy came stumbling beyond the Cadillac.

'Where you been, Pious,' he asked, 'your mama been over here asking?'

Pious was thinking quickly. 'Been down to the landing,' he said, 'figured I ought to check those moorings with the wind blowing like she is.'

'They all right is they?' Albert asked him.

'They is now. Skiff was working loose but I tied her off pretty good. It ain't as sheltered down there as it might be.'

'No it ain't. Anyways your mama been asking.' Albert paused for a moment then he added: 'You-all seen Miss Willow, have you?'

Pious avoided his eye. 'No sir, not since before.'

'Mr Morgan been asking. Come over here just now looking for her but I don't know what he thinks Miss Willow'd be doing in a car garage, it ain't as if she's old enough to be driving.' He shook his head then, gesturing. 'And talking about driving, her mama didn't ought to be on the road neither now that I come to think on it. Not on a night like this, not when she's blowing hard as she is. You-all know what happened to her own mama, don't you?'

'Yes sir, she done wrecked on Bluff Bridge.'

'That's right. She done wrecked on Bluff Bridge and that was twenty years back and that old Ford's still down there.'

———

In his father's study Morgan J was on the telephone. Holding the receiver to his ear he looked across the room to where the old man lay as he had before. His eyes were open, saliva trailing his lip and Morgan J had not taken a tissue to it.

Morgan J's expression was edgy. He gripped the receiver tightly. 'Chase,' he said, 'that brother of yours never was any good. I told you that when you said how we ought to use him.' He cursed then softly. 'So he didn't do what he was told. He didn't even try, is that what you're telling me?' He listened while Chase reported what his brother had related.

'I'll deal with him later,' Morgan J said when he was finished. 'Meantime that leaves us out in the cold.' Again he looked at his father. 'I figure there might be a copy in this room somewhere, but I told you already I can't find it and short of taking the place apart board by board I don't know what else I can do. Trouble is the old man can't tell me even if he wanted to and that only leaves one option.' At the other end of the line Chase was silent. 'Don't go cold on me,' Morgan J warned him; 'not if you want what's coming to you. Can't be a county cop forever and the pension ain't much so they tell me. If you and Peyton want to settle down in Florida there's work still got to be done here.'

———

John Q got the bonds cut finally, working his wrists up and down he sawed away at the baling twine until it frayed and loosened and finally gave out. Hands free, he made short work of his ankles and was on his feet crossing to the patch of peeling wall covering. Reaching inside where it bagged he pulled out the envelope and took a couple of minutes to study the papers. He wasn't one for paperwork particularly, but he knew a little about the law from his Uncle Frank and he could see this was what they called a codicil, an amendment to the last will and testament of Morgan Barra Senior. From what he could see the old man had indeed changed his previous will and left everything to Mrs Flood just as Willow had overheard him tell Morgan Junior.

Folding the papers once more he slipped them back into the envelope and stuffed that inside his shirt. Then he ducked outside where the rain seemed to have abated just a little. Scampering across the open lot he got to the trees where he had left the bicycle. Right now, he figured Noble would be talking on the telephone to Morgan Junior. Having cut his brother out of the deal, he would be trying to sell him the papers. Only he no longer had them to sell. John Q had them and with the rain having eased some, he might make it to his grandma's house before they were so sodden nobody could read them.

As he cycled he was thinking about what Noble had threatened and how he could deal with it if he came along. He was thinking about what his Uncle Frank would do and he was thinking about that '73 Winchester and how he had no shells for it. That didn't matter. His grandma had a twelve gauge she had kept under her bed since her husband went off to war. John Q had grown up with a twelve gauge shotgun; it was the first weapon he had learned how to use back in San Saba County. That was all well and good in his head though, what if it actually came to it?

The thought dried his mouth and, standing on the pedals, he took off across town being careful to keep away from Main Street. He made it as far as the turn onto Riverview Road and as the wind picked up he hunched right over the handlebars.

He got to the house just before the heavens really opened up again, though he was only just in time. Lifting the bicycle onto the porch and dragging his shirt open, he checked the papers and thankfully they were okay. The rain was really coming down again now, rattling off the tin roof overhead but even in the vague light out there he could make out what was written. Inside the house he stood for a moment to catch his breath.

'Is that you, John Q?' His grandma called from her bedroom.

Stuffing the papers back in his shirt once more he made his way along the hallway. 'Yes ma'am,' he said from outside her door.

'Well come on in here a minute so I can talk to you.'

He pushed open the door and she was propped up in bed with her nightgown clasped at the neck and the quilts gathered around her. Laying down her book she studied him with her head to one side. 'So what happened to you?' she asked. 'That's quite the shiner you got building.'

'The rain, Grandma,' he made an open-handed gesture, 'the storm and all. I been riding Pious's bicycle and in the dark I can't see the potholes. Pitched into one and went clear over the handlebars. Guess I must've landed on my noggin.'

Still she looked on, her eyes narrower than they had been. 'Well you want to be more careful,' she stated slowly. 'Where you been, anyway?'

'Just into town, Pious give me a loan of his bicycle.'

From where he stood John Q could see the shotgun lying on the floor under the bed where she could reach it. 'You keep that piece loaded, Grandma?' he asked her.

'Wouldn't be a whole lot of use if I didn't.'

'No ma'am.'

'Why, something I ought to know about is there?'

He bit his lip. 'No ma'am, I was just asking.'

'You don't need to worry on my account,' she told him. 'I been here sixty years already and there ain't much about this county I haven't had to deal with.'

'I know it. I was just asking.'

'Well,' she said, 'go ahead and leave me alone now. I'm done reading, fixing to sleep here in a little bit.'

'Grandma,' he said, 'I been meaning to ask you about that Winchester rifle. I was wondering....'

His grandma pointed through the door to the hallway: 'Box of shells in the closet yonder.'

———

SIXTEEN

Willow did not hear John Q get home. She was in the workshop watching the weather out of the window and thinking that no matter the fears Pious held for her, she could've made the crossing to the island. Standing there she wasn't sure that wasn't what she ought to be doing anyway. She could not stay here all night and she didn't need to wait for John Q. She didn't need to wait for anybody. She was fourteen years old and there was a boat tied up down below and she knew how to start that motor. She could do it, she could navigate the river and she could cross the shoals no matter how hard the wind was blowing.

On the island she would be just fine. There was plenty of water to drink and there was fruit in abundance; she knew what berries to pick and what to leave behind. A person could live on berries or at least they could for a while anyway. She thought of all the places she could hide out, the McElroy house with all those rooms, the cabins at the settlement, not to mention the tunnels under the ruins at Fermanagh.

She still had the oilskin and she unhooked it where she had hung it on the back of the door. Slipping it over her head, she fixed the hood and opened the door and peered out where the rain was falling. Staring across the yard she saw a shadow at the kitchen window and figured it was Grandma Q. Keeping low now she hugged the edge of the lawn till she made the steps to the jetty.

———

John Q had the Winchester laid on the kitchen table and he did not see Willow as she crossed the yard. It was pitch black, the sky thick with rain clouds and not a sink-hole anywhere for a star to peek out or a slice of the moon maybe. The rifle was cleaned and oiled now; the lever mechanism so smooth he could not believe this gun was older than his grandmother.

In the hall he rummaged around in the closet and fetched the box of cartridges. Back in the civil war this was the same type they would've used for the Henry Rifle and John Q knew all about cartridges and calibre because his Uncle Frank had taught him most of it. Rimmed and bottle-necked, the forty-four-forty bullet was almost an inch and a half in length and half an inch in the round. The case was brass and the ball made of lead like always. He worked one between his fingers thinking about what Noble Landry had said about a fillet knife and how he wasn't fifteen years old yet and had never shot anyone.

It wouldn't come to that. Shaking his head he told himself that, for all his threats, Noble wouldn't stoop so low as to use a knife on somebody's grandma and this wouldn't come to anything. But he had to be prepared just in case so he slotted a full fifteen rounds into the Winchester's maga-zine then he laid the gun on the table. Fetching a glass, he poured some milk and his hand shook as he drank it. After that he took the rifle out to the front porch and sat down in his grandma's rocker.

———

In the study Morgan J hung up the phone to Chase Landry. Stepping over to the bed he studied his father with his lips twisted at the corners.

'This is your fault, Dad,' he said. 'You did this; you put me where I'm at right now. It was you brought this down on the household.' Standing there stiff-backed, he gestured. 'What possessed you to adopt her? She was nothing but a squatter for heaven's sake, her mother no better than a whore.'

Eyes cold, his father stared up at him.

'Now I have no option. You left me absolutely no other choice.' Morgan J fell silent for a moment then he added more softly. 'Close your eyes, Daddy. Go ahead and slip away. You don't want to be seeing this any more than I want to be doing it. Either that or point me in the right direction. Show me where the paperwork's at and I won't have to go after either of them.' Again he fell silent. He was thinking. 'Or is the copy with Mortimer the only copy?' He nodded now. 'It is, isn't it: one copy of a will and one copy of the codicil that supersedes it. I mean why would there be two of them? Pity for you that Noble Landry didn't break in there like we told him; pity for Cassie and a real pity for Willow too. Have you seen her, Dad? I can't seem to find her anywhere.'

The phone was ringing again and rather than wait for Mama Sox to pick it up in the hall, Morgan J lifted the receiver. 'This is Morgan Barra Junior.'

For a moment there was silence then a voice spoke in his ear and the accent was not from Georgia. It was east coast all right only further north and it was soft but menacing.

'Morgan J, this is Shoofly and I'm in Spanish Fork right now just down the road from where you're at.'

Morgan J gripped the phone so tightly the blood stopped flowing to his fingers. 'You said a week, Shoofly; you told me I had seven days.'

'Did I say that?'

'You know you did. You told me I had a week.'

'Well if I did, you best think on how I might've changed my mind. I know your old man is sick and all, but I heard how he stopped paying your bills a while back and that set me to thinking. What if you didn't get his money? What if he don't trust you not to blow it? I mean how long's it been since he started bailing you out and how long since he thought better of it? They tell me you got six months owing on the Grand Hotel and that don't include the whiskey.' He sighed then. 'Old Shoofly's a cautious soul, Morgan J; all his life people done told him how he's a thinker and he got to thinking how maybe you just won't be able to pay him.'

'Of course I'll be able to pay. I told you as soon as the old man's gone I'm going to be worth a fortune.'

'Yeah that's what you told me, but old Shoofly started thinking how it was that a shrewd old buzzard like Dandy Nichols wanted to sell a Barra note for only seventy-cents on the dollar.'

Morgan J could hear him breathing.

'I guess all that thinking done made me nervous so I figured I'd swing on down here and visit with you just so's you could assure me that you will have what you owe.'

He paused then and Morgan J sent his tongue across his lips to try and moisten them.

'So go ahead, Morgan J. Assure me.'

————

Noble Landry was in the lobby and he could see a black man in the only telephone booth they had. He was sitting with his back to the glass door talking into the handset. Noble was irritated suddenly, all the time that phone was occupied he was stuck here and he knew that kid would be busting a gut to get quit of the baling twine.

Finally the black guy hung up and got to his feet and pushed open the folding doors. He came out brushing long fingers across the brim of his fedora. Two heavy looking goons who had been lounging just inside the main doors were on their feet as he crossed the floor. Briefly he exchanged a glance with Noble then fitted his hat on his head and one of the goons threw a top coat around his shoulders while Noble stood there with a single dime stamped against his palm. He wore the ratty old oilskin that had belonged to his father. His shoes leaked, his trousers did not fit and everybody knew how he lived in a derelict Pullman.

Finally, he was in the booth with the doors closed. He took a seat and slotted his dime. The operator came on the line and he told her to connect him with the Barra House at Spanish Bluff. Sounding a little suspicious, she asked him who was calling.

That about finished him: 'Tell them it's Noble Landry,' he stated. 'Morgan Junior wants to talk to me.'

———

Willow got down to Grandma Q's jetty just as the wind sent the wash rolling in a three foot wave upriver. For a moment she hesitated. She looked back up the flight of steps and thought about returning to the workshop. But what was the point in that, she had come this far and she backed herself to make it across to the island. Getting aboard the little skiff Pious had piloted, she took a long look at the motor. It was an Evinrude and she knew it was a little more-fiddley than the seahorse her mother had bought, but she had watched Pious start it when they left the lagoon. She had a flashlight she had found in the workshop and inspecting the workings now she recalled how the magneto had to be set and together with the primer. That done she looped the rope coil around the starter and hauled on it.

Her face creased in a smile as the engine fired and the outboard sent a torrent of gray foam burbling beyond the propeller. Sitting back now she eased the boat away from the mooring and swung it around and it was so dark she could barely see anything. The river cut a cleft in the land here and, with the steeply rising banks, even in the daytime there was not much sunlight. It didn't matter; it was pitch-dark right now and Willow could negotiate this river on instinct.

Even so the wind blew hard in her face, the bows lifting to rear up like a horse and for a moment that worried her. In all her years crossing to the island she had never felt the water so restless. Ignoring her nerves though, she threaded a path all the way out to where fresh water met the salt. Here the world seemed lighter, lighter and a whole lot rougher. On the lip of The Dividing the boat was kicked around like it was made of balsa wood and Willow could see the height of the swell where the tides clashed above the hidden sandbars. That water was chopped and broken; it was a mass of darkened motion. She realised that she had never been out in anything like this and for all her bravado it seemed suddenly very foolish.

It was too late though, already she was in the bay and there was no turning back and she thought of all those sharks just waiting for the boat to flip over. Her father once told her that after the great white and tiger, the bull shark was the most dangerous in the sea. She tried not to think about it. She told herself that though this was a very small boat she knew what she was doing and she could make it across to the island.

She steered out into the bay. With the waves thrashing the hull she jogged west of the entrance to the Orange Blossom River and there the swell was incredible; one minute the boat was riding high and the next it was cowering in sloughs of water that threatened to swamp her. The slower she went the worse it was and, winding on the power, she headed for the passage between the sandbars.

She started to zigzag as she knew had to, but with the wind as it was the little boat was rolling and it was all she could do to try and keep the bows angled correctly. The skiff was pitching and yawing; the hull scraping where it wallowed yet somehow she managed to keep from grounding. Beyond the shoals she was in deep water again and she motored hard till she was in the lee of Cooper's Bluff. There the wind dropped a little in its intensity.

She had not made it yet though, not by a long way. All she had managed so far was to cross the shoals and there was plenty open water ahead and she was not sure she could navigate that with the waves as high as they were. Her course was northeast and as she eased beyond the shelter of Cooper's Bluff the wind slapped the starboard side of the boat with such force it shuddered right through her. Directly north was Bull Shark Bay, that massive hole in the sea bed where the sharks gathered in the greatest numbers. The last thing Willow wanted to do was to end up there in this kind of weather, it was bad enough in the calm. She knew she couldn't risk being pushed too far north, not with the way the wind was, and a few hundred yards further she turned east for the Jabberwock.

A series of rivulets; narrow channels that, from the hilltop, looked just like the Jabberwock's elongated neck, its skinny limbs and bat-like wings.

Years ago Mama Sox had shown her a picture. There was so much silt in the water it was not a place to fall in because although the Jabberwock's arms were shallow enough, they were laced with mud that would grab you by the ankles and suck you under. Willow had to find her way through that maze with only the flashlight to guide her. Get it wrong and the boat would stick on the float top or flounder in the marsh itself where it could easily be tipped over.

She was working the engine as her mother had taught her, easing on and off the throttle, checking opening after opening, waterway after waterway and so many of them dead ends. She made a mistake here another there, taking the wrong channel before realizing it and turning the boat around.

On and on she journeyed, shifting the little craft this way and that, it seemed to take an age, the wind in her face and the surface of the marshy water broken up by the rain. Finally she was through and once again she was back in open water. It was slacker here though, and the run was short to the Narrows. Her heart began to leap as she realized she was almost there. From the Narrows it was the lagoon and the beach and the settlement.

But she was not safe yet and the tide was shifting one way with the wind driving the other and between the two the tiny boat was teetering on the brink of disaster.

Halfway across that last stretch the engine coughed and stalled and Willow hit the revs to bring it back but it coughed again and then again before it puttered into stillness. She sat there with her hand on the tiller and her heart in her mouth and the skiff now drifting wildly.

She had no control. Already the current was dragging her around and with the wind from the southeast she knew it would propel her into Bull Shark Bay. If she capsized there it would be the end of everything. Reaching for the rope pull on top of the engine she unsettled the stern, a wave hit and the boat flipped over.

———

SEVENTEEN

Unaware of Willow's plight her mother drove back to Spanish Fork for the second time in just a few hours. The little Ford convertible had the headlights working overtime in order that she could see the road ahead where the rain swept and the wind blew and the trees seemed to billow either side.

She had managed to get the blood thinning drugs the doctor did not have. She had been to the hospital and now she needed to get them home as quickly as possible. She drove sitting hunched against the steering wheel, her back stiff and her eyes sharp because the storm had barely brushed Rutherford but was as bad here as it had been on the journey west.

Only one road, it was narrow and winding as it cut across hillsides where the woodland dominated. There was some asphalt stretches to the road but mostly it was hard packed gravel and it was there Cassie was at her most vulnerable. With the rain coming down all day the road could wash out anytime and take her car along with it.

She drove quickly but carefully, as good behind the wheel of a car as she was at the tiller of a boat. She knew this road. Willow went to school in Rutherford. When they had lived in Savannah she had boarded the entire term but after her father was killed they wanted to spend weekends together so Cassie drove her over on a Sunday and picked her up again on Friday.

Inside her head the doctor's words echoed; how it was that her grandpa needed the drugs, how there had been no point in sending for an ambulance because the journey to the hospital would've killed him. She imagined Mama Sox's fright when she found him. The poor woman had only just moved into the apartment and before tonight Cassie had never seen her happier.

She had known Mama all her life. Only ten years old when Cassie was born, Mama had assisted in the birth, boiled water and fetched towels for Mrs Q was how she told it. For the first five years of Cassie's life the woman who was now her housekeeper had been like a big sister.

Cassie recalled how her mother had been in those days, thick-skinned and capable of most anything; ignoring all the jibes, the comments thrown at them whenever they crossed The Dividing. She had been as good a mother as a mother could be and when Morgan J was knocking back the whiskey that summer she had never seen her mother touch a single drop.

She drove on, concentrating on the road now but with Morgan J on her mind suddenly. His presence in the house always bothered her but this time it was particularly loathsome because she knew he was only there because his father was dying and the house and island would be coming to him. Finally he could build whatever he wanted. He could knock down the McElroy place and raze the settlement. He could have his damned marina.

She pushed the thoughts away, aware that her mind was wandering and that would not do. She had to concentrate, the rain falling ever more heavily and the wind growing wilder. She realised just how tightly her fingers were wrapped around the steering wheel and she relaxed a little, sat back a little, didn't hunch so much: she had a pain in her back from hunching.

Rounding a bend she had to stamp hard on the brake. The road was out, fallen trees blocking the way; a great mass of earth and tree roots stretching from the woods on one side all the way to the other. She was still going pretty quickly and the back end of the convertible slewed on its skinny tires. The wheel seemed to come alive under her palms but she controlled it and brought the car to a stop.

For a moment she just sat there. There was no way past; the landslide covered the whole of the road and she did not know what to do. She did not know whether to get out or sit there. With the headlights shining she could see where a great swathe of earth had slipped from the hillside. The wind, the weight of the water, it had collapsed the trees, sent them across the highway dragging mud and stones and debris. There was no way past and she was still miles from Spanish Fork and her grandpa needed the medicine. Suddenly she was panicking. She did not know what to do. Her grandpa needed those drugs to keep his blood thin because it could clot again any time and another stroke would kill him.

——

Noble put down the phone on Morgan Junior and as he stepped out of the booth he had a smug little smile on his face. The desk clerk looked up briefly as he sauntered onto Main Street. Glancing across the road he saw a Chevy Sedan with white walled tires and the three black guys from the hotel sitting inside. The one with the hat was in the back; the two goons up front and Noble wondered what a group like that were doing there.

Crossing the street, he headed south for the railroad car that had been his home since he had been released from the workhouse. It would not be home much longer. With the deal he had just cut he could leave that place and get quit of the county and that's what he planned to do. He felt bad about having to tie that kid up and he felt bad about the threat he'd made about Grandma Q. He might have spent plenty of time in the workhouse but the only occasion he had ever hurt anyone was in Europe during the war. It was on account of his brother he'd ended up this way and he hated him for that. But Chase was no longer in the picture and he was dealing directly with Morgan Junior. An option; that's what this new situation gave him and Noble had not had one of those in a long time.

The rain was falling as heavily now as at any time during the day. It was a while since they had had this kind of storm and he tried to imagine being out on the water in that little row boat he had rented from Lenny. Crossing the square he walked past the statue of Light Horse Harry Lee. He walked beyond Lenny's place and the grocery store. After that he was in the sort of no man's land just north of the railroad tracks and there was the open lot and the Pullman.

Shaking the rain from his shoulders he went inside. 'Hey kid,' he called, 'I guess we're all done now and if you keep your trap shut I might just let you go.'

No answer. No movement. His eyes narrowed. 'Kid,' he said, pacing the length of the car. 'I said I might just.......' He stood there looking down at the tick of a mattress where the old blanket he had traded for was thrown back and there was no sign of the boy. Gazing the length of the car once more, he spotted strands of baling twine right by the door. In a flash he was at the peeling wall paper rooting around where it bagged, but the makeshift pouch was empty.

———

Up at the house, Morgan J walked the landing to Willow's bedroom. Knocking once he opened the door.

'Are you in here, Willow?' he called.

She did not answer and he stepped into the room and took a look around. The bed was turned back but there was no sign of the girl. He checked the bathroom but she wasn't there.

'Where'd you get to?' It was a murmur; he was talking to himself now considering the room, how neat and pretty it was though in reality she had no business being there. Her mother had no business being there, she never had and the fact she was here had kept him away from this place for as long as he could remember.

But it no longer mattered. That phone call had changed everything and there was more to Noble Landry than he would've figured. Noble was smarter than his brother actually, but then smart wasn't something Morgan needed in Chase, obedience with him was everything.

On the landing he stood for a moment resting his hand on the banister. This house would be sold, too much of his father here and he had never liked it anyway. He would buy a smaller place if he bought anywhere around here at all. He would keep the island though, that was a gold mine waiting to be harvested.

Thinking about his plans brought him back to Shoofly, how that gangster had travelled all the way down from New Jersey on a word from someone at the Grand Hotel. Well Morgan J would not be going back to the hotel. He would not be going back to Atlantic City. With his inheritance intact he had no need of the tables anymore, his gamble would be the island and the development plans he had had since he was twenty. His confidence was growing now and as far as Shoofly was concerned, he started thinking of how certain people round here would take to the idea of a black man putting the squeeze on him.

——

Willow was underwater. The oilskin clustered about her head threatening to drag her down and desperately she tried to shake off the garment. Coming up for air beside the capsized boat she could breathe if only for a moment. She felt the whiplash of rain on her face. She heard the wind howl and the sea itself seemed to roar in her ears like the roaring of the whirlpool where her grandmother had died all those years before. Sucked under again she was just able to gulp enough of a breath and below the waves she fought to take hold of the panic. Somehow she managed to strip away first one sleeve of the oilskin and then the other and finally she surfaced.

She breathed. She swam. For all she was worth she swam now. All she could think about were those sharks, hundreds of them hunting ceaselessly. The thought stilled her heart and she kicked for the narrows and the slack water of the lagoon that came after.

All the way the waves bullied her; they toyed with her, fooled her into thinking she might make it. Sucking great lungfuls of air she was under the water and above it again telling herself she could make it. She would make it. She swam harder and harder, conscious that if she could just get across that final stretch the current would subside and she would be in the Narrows. There, as in the arms of the Jabberwock, the passage was shallow but unlike the Jabberwock the floor of the channels had been packed hard by millions of oyster shells that had long since fused together. There was no silt in the Narrows. In the Narrows she had a chance and she swam with every ounce of strength she could muster.

All the way she could feel imaginary sharks bumping their snouts against her legs and nibbling at her feet threatening to bite great chunks out of her. But no sharks came and finally she felt the current loosen and she could smell mud in the water. She was up to her chin, the oyster shell bottom just about underfoot; she was bobbing momentarily on tiptoe. She was among the reeds where sections of marsh had broken away in little islands and here the wind passed overhead and there was no current and though she had lost the boat, she had made it without drowning.

Beyond the Narrows she was on the rocks and then in the lagoon. Calm water, the surface only ruffled by the wind. Finally she made the beach, the last few yards she was swimming then she felt the sea bed under her toes and she was paddling and stumbling and paddling again. Not quite believing she had made it, she collapsed onto hard, cold sand and she lay with her cheek against it and her breath coming in desperate gasps. She lay there both relieved and exhilarated. Not only had she survived the boat going over, she had swum the channel and the narrows and finally the lagoon. She was cold though, she was freezing cold and she was exhausted.

On her feet, it was all she could do to stand for a moment before she collapsed on the sand once more. Her legs buckled under her and she sat there supporting her weight with her hands. Head tipped back she looked into the dark of the sky and the rain fell harsh across the skin of her face.

She was shivering and something told her she could not afford to stay there any longer. She really did have to get up and she had to do it now. It was a monumental effort but somehow she managed and this time she stayed on her feet and tottered along the windblown shore.

Finally she got to the trees and she could make out the rickety old jetty the islanders had built back when her mother was a girl. Her mother, she thought about how she was driving back from Rutherford with the medicine her great-grandpa needed. She thought about what she had heard Morgan Junior say when she had been hiding under the bed. Her mother had no idea she was in danger. Her mother had no idea what had happened and what it meant to Morgan J. In a panic now Willow gazed the width of the channel and wondered what she had been thinking about when she decided to make this crossing.

She thought about Pious. Pious said he would tell her mother what had happened and her mother would know what to do. But then Pious thought she was hiding in the workshop at Grandma Q's house and it was Grandma Q's skiff she had taken. If those tides did not swamp it the boat would be washed upriver to wreck somewhere on the banks. They would think she had drowned and she couldn't bear the thought of her mother believing she was lying at the bottom of the ocean.

There was nothing she could do about it though, nothing at all. She knew she had to push those thoughts away and concentrate on getting out of the storm. With no boat she was trapped here until somebody made the crossing. Until then she had to keep her mind on her situation and not worry about what was going on over on the mainland: more than anything she had to take shelter from this storm.

———

On the road east from Rutherford her mother climbed out of the car. The downed trees were not going anywhere, neither was that mound of earth and that meant neither was she. She still had the engine running and the headlights formed a pale wash across the landslide where she could see there were no breaks, no way to get the car through. There was no other road. There was no traffic out here, no other automobile and she had only seen a handful of trucks since she left Rutherford. It was too wild a night to be driving. Anyone who knew anything about this part of the country knew how these storms could be.

She stood there with the rain falling and the wind tearing at her hair. She could turn the car around and drive back to Rutherford or she could stay here. No, she could not stay here, that was ridiculous. To sit in the car all night would be foolish because in the morning, even if the storm had subsided, the road would still be blocked. She would have to wait until a crew from the county had been out to clear it and they would not necessarily know it was blocked. Not unless somebody told them. That somebody had to be her.

She was about to turn the car around when she saw a set of lights shining suddenly from further down the road. Beyond where the trees were felled the highway stretched arrow straight for a mile or more and she could see a pair of headlights coming this way. Another car, it would arrive at the far side of the downed trees and with no way through it would have to turn around and go back the same way. Cassie's heart started thumping as she realised she had a chance of getting the medication back to the house after all. She had tears in her eyes as she scrambled back to the car. The paper sack she had been given at the hospital was in the glove box and she reached for it now.

The approaching vehicle was getting closer all the time. Making her way around the landslip, Cassie climbed over fallen trees until she was on the eastern side and she waited, trying to keep the sack out of the rain.

The car was making very slow progress; barely creeping along where the highway had been turned to mud. Still it pressed on though, and as it got closer Cassie could see not only the twin headlights, but a single red light on the roof. That was a police car, a county sheriff's cruiser; a Light

Horse County Deputy. Her heart leapt as she realised she could get them to take her home. She was a Barra and when she told them she had drugs for Morgan Senior they would hit that light and siren.

She waved now, one hand clutching the paper sack. The car was almost to the point where the road was blocked and she could see how the tires were hardly gripping at all. They must have spotted her standing there and they came on and on until finally the car pulled up. Cassie stepped towards them, her footing unsure in the mud. The driver's door opened and she was about to call out when a man's voice lifted through the rain.

'Mrs Flood, is that you?'

Chase Landry, Cassie remembered him as a young deputy back when she was a child. She remembered Peyton Skipwith, the way those two would look at her; the way they looked at her still. She did not answer. For some reason she could not find her voice. She did not know why but something made her falter.

'Mrs Flood,' Chase called again. 'Is that you over there? What happened, ma'am?' Did you wreck your car?'

At the sound of those words Cassie felt every muscle in her body go stiff. Eyes closed she was at Bluff Bridge and the memorial service for her mother where she tossed flowers into the waters of The Pit below.

———

EIGHTEEN

John Q sat in his grandma's rocking chair with the rifle across his knees and fifteen rounds loaded, though he was yet to slot one in the chamber. The weapon had a saddle ring on the breech and he toyed with it as a way of distracting his thoughts from the nerves that were gathered in his stomach.

He could hear someone walking in the rain. The wind had dipped just a fraction but sitting out here for the last half-hour he had gotten used to it and had been picking up other sounds; night birds, bats, all kinds of stuff he figured he would not be able to hear on account of the weather. But he could hear them and those were footsteps now for sure.

In silhouette Noble appeared at the gate. John Q had the light switched out on the porch and he was sitting off to the left so Noble would not automatically set eyes on him when he himself came into view. John Q could hear him curse as he fumbled with the gate. It had stuck a little since he had painted it and he'd meant to take the wet and dry to a spot right by the latch but hadn't gotten round to it yet.

Noble had the gate open. He was on the path heading for the porch, cursing softly under his breath.

'That'll do right there.' John Q barely trusted his voice. Not knowing what else to do he did his best to sound brave and spoke from where he was hidden in the shadows still. He was aware of just how fast his heart was beating and how his palms were sweating so much he could barely keep hold of the gun.

On the path Noble froze mid-step.

Getting up now John Q moved to where he could be seen and he had the Winchester levelled and he was not fifteen years old and had never pointed a rifle at anyone. When his Uncle Frank first showed him how to use one he told him how he was never to point it at another human being unless he meant to shoot them. It was a lesson learned well and even with weapon he knew was empty he had never done it. But this was a '73 Winchester and it was loaded all right and it was aimed at Noble Landry.

Noble looked up at him and through the gloom now John Q could just about make out his features.

'What do you think you're doing, kid, pointing a gun at me?'

'Well,' John Q could hear the way his voice was wavering. 'I'm doing it on account of how it was my grandma you told me you'd be whetting your knife on.'

'Oh come on,' Noble flapped a palm at him. 'That was just talk and you know it. I ain't never took a knife to nobody and I ain't about to start now, least of all with your grandma.' He sniffed then, wiped a hand across his face in the rain. 'I tell you what: you-all go ahead and give me back those papers you stole and I won't worry about how you dragged me all the way out here. I'll head on back and we don't need to be talking to anybody about nothing and we don't need to set eyes on each other again.'

'Can't do it,' John Q told him. 'You stole those papers, Noble: broke into the attorney's office without he'd know you'd been there. You told me that yourself.'

'So, what's it to you? You done stole them from me.'

'I ain't sure I stole them exactly. I mean they'd already been stole and they ain't yours anyways. I figure I took them for safe-keeping.'

'Is that what you figure you did?' the sarcasm was dripping now.

'You aim to sell them to Morgan Junior,' John Q told him. 'He'll burn them most probably, destroy them and then all what Mr Barra meant for Willow's momma will go to him.'

'I don't care what he does with them. I just aim to get them to him.' Noble took another step towards the porch. 'Right about now he's on his way over to my railroad car and he's going to be pissed when he don't find me back there so I don't got time for this. Go ahead now and fetch me the papers.'

'Can't do it,' John Q repeated. 'I figure if Morgan J gets them then Willow and her momma are probably going to end up homeless or something and that ain't how their grandpa wants it at all.'

Noble laughed softly. 'Kid,' he said. 'Did it not occur to you that without them papers Morgan J won't just be making them homeless? Didn't you hear what Chase and Peyton said?'

Through the shadows John Q stared at him.

'You didn't get that part figured then.' Heartened maybe, Noble took another pace towards him now. 'Well here's how it is. Morgan J needs his inheritance. He needs his old man's property and he's going to get it any which-way because it rightly belongs to him.'

'Noble, his daddy ain't dead yet and he don't see it that way.'

'Not yet he ain't dead maybe, but I heard how he's had a stroke and can't talk and just lies there dribbling. He's a sick old man and he ain't got long and there ain't no way Morgan J's going to let money he's got coming go to no squatter's kid.' He gestured then. 'Come ahead with the papers now. You got no business being involved here and you got no business with that rifle.'

'And you got no business being on my property.' The voice came from the path to the side of the house and John Q started as suddenly as Noble did. His grandma in her nightgown, she was pale like a ghost only this spectre was carrying a twelve gauge shotgun.

Noble stared at her and she came forward with the hammers cocked and both barrels aimed at him.

'Johnny, put up that Winchester,' she told him. 'You're too young to be pointing it.'

John Q hesitated.

'Go ahead and do as I tell you. I got this weasel covered.'

John Q put the gun up.

'That shiner ain't anything to do with tumbling off a bicycle now, is it?'

'No ma'am, I guess it ain't.'

'Don't like being lied to, son; but seeing as we got this little contretemps going on I figure you probably thought you had good reason.' She jerked the gun at Noble. 'Best you come in the house, Noble Landry. Time we got to the bottom of what-all's going on here and I'm too old to be doing that in a rainstorm.'

———

Willow was inside the hut where Mama Sox had grown up and she was finally out of the storm. She was still cold though, she was shivering and she had no matches and there was no wood to build a fire. She had no blanket, only the clothes she stood up in and they were so wet still they were sticking to her. Her teeth were chattering, she could not make them stop and she knew that somehow she had to get warm.

There was no light and she had to move about the cabin by touch. Slowly however, her eyes did get accustomed to the gloom. She could make out a little rough furniture, a chair perhaps and some kind of table. The hut was comprised of two rooms with a sort of arch between them and as far as she could tell the back room was empty.

She sat down on the chair, her shirt clammy against her skin and her britches sticking to her. She had taken her pumps off now and she was barefoot and her toes felt frozen. Still she shivered and she hugged herself as she huddled there listening to the rain.

———

Her mother was in the back seat of the deputies' Ford. Only two doors, Chase Landry had to flip the seat forward so she could climb in and as she did that she saw the way he seemed to peer at her.

'Are you all right, Mrs Flood?' Settling in the driver's seat once more, he hunched round with his arm on the back. 'What're you doing all the way out here?'

It occurred to Cassie that she might ask him the same question. There were plenty of sheriff's deputies to cover the county so what were he and Peyton doing so far from home? Her heart began to thump a little as she thought about it but she held his eye though she was no longer sure she should have got in this car at all.

'My grandfather's had a stroke,' she told him. 'The doctor didn't want him moved so I drove to Rutherford to get some drugs he needs from the hospital.'

Sitting in the passenger seat Peyton seemed to study her carefully; jowly and bug-eyed, he worked a palm across the bristles on his chin.

'What kind of drugs, ma'am?' he asked her.

'Drugs to keep his blood thin.'

'Really; I ain't never heard of that.'

'No, neither had I before today, but then I'm no doctor.'

'Nope, I guess I ain't either. Can do a little first aid,' Peyton gestured, 'goes with the job on account of how it's usually us first on the scene whenever a car gets wrecked.'

Cassie stared at him, trying to work out what was going on behind those bug-eyes. 'Is that what you're doing all the way out here?' she asked. 'I've never seen you this far west.'

'No ma'am,' Chase said. 'It wasn't a wreck brought us out here. Told us on the radio just now how some fella escaped from the truck leaving out for the workhouse and how he'd been spotted on this here highway. Seeing as we were already in Miller's Town we said we'd see if we couldn't track the sucker down.'

He started the engine and Cassie felt her muscles begin to unravel a fraction. She tried to relax. She had no reason to mistrust them, those feelings she had had just now were only on account of what they said had happened to her mother. But that was years ago.

Chase backed up and swung the car around and they drove back the way they had come. From the back seat Cassie watched the windshield where the rain lashed and the wipers could barely cope. The headlamps made little impression on the darkness and this section of highway was narrower than it was closer to Rutherford. Almost a single lane in places, it only got narrower the closer it got to the coast.

So much mud under the wheels she could feel how the tires were not coping and in places there was no grip at all. Chase had to fight hard with the wheel and cursing under his breath, finally he turned to his partner.

'Can't see how we're going to make it,' he said, 'not when she's storming like this, can't get no purchase from the tires at all.'

Behind him Cassie sat forward. 'We have to make it,' she said, 'my grandfather needs those meds.'

'I know that. I hear you.' Chase glanced in the mirror. 'But you can see the kind of progress we're making. You can see how the road is up ahead.' He lifted a palm. 'Already got trees down, that's why you're setting where you're at.' He looked sideways at Peyton. 'See there's a turnout yonder. I figure we need to set tight for a moment and see if we can't think this through.'

'No,' Cassie objected. 'We can't do that. We have to keep going. My grandpa could die if I don't get the medicine back to him.'

'Yes he could,' again Chase looked at her in the mirror, 'but if a tree comes down right here then so could we and I ain't about to risk my life on account of it and neither is Peyton.'

———

Pious was in the garage when Morgan J came over from the house. Albert had gone to bed and Pious had been up to check on his sister but she was sleeping now and pretty soon his mother would be home. He had just come down again when Morgan J crunched across the driveway.

When he saw Pious his eyes narrowed sharply. 'What're you doing here? Boy your age, isn't it time you were upstairs already?'

'Yes sir it is and I'm going up now.' Pious went to step past him but Morgan J settled a hand on his shoulder. 'I asked you what you were doing here.'

'I was just checking everything was all right with the garage doors,' Pious told him. 'I know how Albert likes to keep them open all the time because he figures closed doors don't do much for the paintwork on those automobiles. That's just fine I guess, but garage doors let the rainwater in and rainwater ain't exactly good for the paintwork neither.'

'What're you talking about?' Morgan J cocked his head to one side.

'Albert got a point I suppose,' Pious went on, 'I heard it said that a car needs to breathe good clean air and not all just when she's moving.'

Shaking his head Morgan J looked the length of his nose at him. 'Boy, I have no idea what you're babbling about but I haven't got time for it now.' With that he got behind the wheel of the Cadillac.

Pious climbed the steps to the apartment and as he did his mother came out of the kitchen. Crossing to the garage she was almost run over by Morgan J.

'What's he doing,' she said, 'Pious, where's Mr Morgan going in this kind of weather?'

'I don't know, Mama. He never said.'

Morgan J swung the car around and with gravel hissing from under the tires he sped off down the driveway.

Looking on in disgust, Mama Sox wagged her head. 'His father sick as he is and him taking off like that, I don't know, I swear. Don't understand some folks, don't understand them at all.' She looked up at Pious once more. 'Is Eunice asleep already?'

'Yes'm she is.'

'All right then. I'm going to have to set with Mr Barra till Mr Morgan gets back because somebody got to look out for him. Come over now with me, Pious, you can help fix up his bed.' She clicked her tongue. 'That poor man, can't be left on his own, not the way he's so sick and all and his own son won't be there for him. I swear I don't know what it is with that one. Always been like it but that don't excuse it. Never did.'

Inside the big house they shook the rain from their clothes then Mama Sox went to the fridge and fetched a pitcher of milk.

She poured Pious a tall glass. 'You ain't had no supper have you, boy; neither you nor Miss Willow. Where's she got to in this weather with her mama on the road like she is?'

Pious did not say anything.

'I don't know what this house is coming to, no sooner does we get moved out of south city and it all seems to fall to bits. Where's she at, Pious; where's Miss Willow hiding herself?'

Pious shrugged his shoulders.

Mama Sox clicked her tongue. 'Well she better show up before her momma gets home because I swear, I ain't going to answer for it if she don't.'

She led him to the study where she knocked on the door. There was no reply of course, and she poked her head around then beckoned Pious to follow. He had never been in the study. He had never been in the big house till just now and until Albert drove them out from south city he hadn't been to Spanish Bluff at all. Now he was in Mr Barra's study where the old man was lying in a bed they had fixed up because he could no longer make the stairs.

Hands clasped Mama Sox went over to him and when she spoke her voice was low.

'Mr Barra, sir,' she said, 'Mr Morgan done gone out somewheres so I brought my boy to help me get you settled. Need to get you settled for the night, sir; need to get you your sleep so you got your strength because I'm sure you is going to be a whole lot better come the morning. I can't do that by myself so I hope you don't mind how I brung my boy.'

For a moment the old man looked at her then his gaze flitted to Pious who turned his attention to the floor. He stood there under the scrutiny, felt the weight of that gaze and he thought about what Willow had said. He found himself looking up again and he held the old man's eye. Mr Barra stared at him and then his gaze rolled around to his mother and Mama Sox slipped a palm underneath his head.

'Need to fix up these pillows for you, sir,' she told him. 'Need to settle this bed.'

She had Pious hold him upright while she puffed up his pillows and straightened the sheet as best she could. It wasn't enough though, the bottom sheet was all rumpled up where he was lying still and she could see he would never be comfortable.

'Mr Barra,' she said. 'If it's all right, sir, we're going to lift you out of this bed.'
Slowly the old man blinked at her.

'Pious, you're going to have to help me,' his mother told him. She pointed to the armchair. 'Bring that close now so Mr Barra got someplace to sit. Then I want you to take his legs and I'll take him under the shoulders.'

'You'll hurt your back, Mama,' Pious told her. 'Let me do it, I'm pretty strong. I reckon I can lift him by myself.'

His mother drew the covers back and the old man lay there in his nightshirt. Very carefully, Pious slid one arm around his back and the other under his legs and he was so thin and frail he was lifted easily. Pious held him, Mr Barra looking into his face and again Pious thought he could see something in his eyes and he understood what Willow had been talking about. Carefully, he settled him in the chair and placed a blanket around him while his mother fixed up the bed.

Now the old man seemed to be straining. His mouth open, lips hung with specks of saliva; his eyes were sharp and they seemed to be trying to communicate. Pious stared at him. He wanted to speak, to ask him what it was he wanted but the old man couldn't talk and his mother would chastise him for speaking out of turn.

'Miss Willow is just fine, sir,' he said it anyway, thinking that's what was worrying the old man. 'She ain't here right now, but she's okay.'

Still Mr Barra stared at him with that same expression in his eyes and his mother looked round from where she was straightening the bed.

'What-all are you saying?'

'I'm just saying to Mr Barra how Miss Willow is okay.'

'Did he ask you? I never heard him; did he ask you to talk out of turn like that?'

'I ain't talking out of turn, Mama; it's just the way he's looking at me.'

'Well, it ain't your place to be saying how Mr Barra is looking at you and it ain't your place to be thinking how there's things he might want said.'

She had the bed straight, the sheets smooth and the pillow cases. She told him to lift the old man again and lay him down very gently. Pious did that, he picked him up as he might a child and for a moment the old man's mouth was right by his ear. 'Grandma Q,' he whispered.

Two words, nothing but the thinnest kind of sound and Pious wondered if he had felt them rather than heard them. Whichever it was he was aware of a little shiver working through him and carefully he laid the old man back down. Now Pious looked closely at his face.

'Grandma Q, did you say, Mr Barra?'

A light seemed to spark in the old man's eyes, his expression seemed to ease and Pious was certain he had heard him as he thought he did.

'What's that?' his mother said to him. 'What you saying about Grandma Q?'

Still Pious was looking at Mr Barra. 'Nothing, Mama; it ain't anything.'

'Pious Noon,' she said, 'if you're going to speak in riddles then don't be speaking at all. You ain't making no sense tonight, I think this storm done gone to your head.' Straightening the top cover finally she looked down at the bed. 'I'm going to be just back there in the kitchen, sir,' she said. 'I'll look in on you every half hour to make sure you're all right.' She turned to Pious then. 'You run along now you hear. I didn't bring Eunice all the way out here just for that girl to spend all night by herself. Go on back upstairs, Pious. I'll be along in a piece.'

———

NINETEEN

John Q was seated at the kitchen table between Noble Landry and his grandmother who had the codicil to Morgan Barra's will spread before her and the shotgun across her lap.

Noble had crumbled. Whatever kind of resolve he thought he might have had in coming here, it had fallen to pieces when he was faced by an old woman in her nightgown sporting a shotgun. Listening to him trying to explain himself John Q wasn't sure if he was just squirming or actually meant what he said. He seemed to mean it, saying how he was sorry for tying him up and everything but it was all on account of his brother Chase.

He made no move to try and grab the codicil, though that might have something to do with the twelve-gauge of course. He sounded thoroughly miserable, explaining how he'd had no place to live since he had gotten back from the war in Europe; how he was supposed to have had a room with his brother's family but that hadn't worked out. He told them how the only money he could earn was what he could catch in fish.

He told them how his brother had made a lot of deals down the years that didn't fit with his status as a sheriff's deputy, how usually he got dragged into them and it was him who took the fall if things went wrong. He had never spoken out against Chase before now because of what he was capable of. Earlier that evening John Q had witnessed the kind of trouble he could bring. Noble explained that the only reason he had agreed to break into the attorneys' office at all was because he needed money so badly and Chase had him over a barrel on account of Lenny's boat.

'But you told him you'd never been in the office at all and thought you'd broker something with Morgan J yourself,' Grandma Q's expression was sour. 'Scheming like that, it don't matter how poor a man is, Noble that ain't where he ought to be at.' She studied the papers again. 'Says here how Morgan J is cut out of his inheritance.'

'Yes ma'am,' Noble nodded. 'His father went and left every penny to Mrs Flood. That's why Morgan J wants the papers. He figures that the original will must still be lodged someplace and all he has to do is destroy what you got there and everything goes back to how it was.'

Glancing across the table she squinted at him. 'What's going to happen when the lawyer opens up his office in the morning and this ain't where it's supposed to be at?'

'He ain't going to know. I done picked that lock and sprung her again when I left out. No fixings on the file cabinet; he ain't going to notice nothing till the old man croaks and then he's going to figure he mislaid it or something I guess. Besides,' he said, 'that envelope was sealed so it's a fact he probably don't know what was in there anyhow.' He sat forward then. 'Look, I know how I done wrong and everything but it's like I told your boy, that paperwork is all that stands between Mrs Flood and a hole in the ground someplace and that goes for her little'un too.'

Uneasily John Q shifted his weight. 'I figure Noble's right about that, Grandma. You should've heard what those deputies said.'

She looked briefly at him then. 'Where are they now, Noble?' she asked. 'Where are Chase and Peyton at?'

Shrugging his shoulders, Noble shook his head.

'Grandma,' John Q stated. 'Chase doesn't know that Noble really does have the papers and I figure he'll have told that to Morgan J. Chances are that would've been before Noble called him up on the phone.' He looked at Noble again. 'I figure Morgan J already sent those two off on the only other option he figures he's got.' His eyes widened as the implication of his words came home. 'Right now Willow's mother is on her way back from

Rutherford on account of how she had to get medicine from the hospital. Night like this when it's storming and trees are coming down all the time, how easy would it be to wreck?'

———

Pious left his mother and went to check on his sister. Eunice was sleeping soundly though, so grabbing the oilskin he ran the length of the yard. Slithering down the wooden steps he was at the landing where the river seemed just a little quieter now. In the boat he fired up the motor and pulled out into the current. Opening the throttle the bows lifted and he rode the waves hard to John Q's landing.

There was no skiff tied up at the mooring. The first thing he noticed when he got around the last bend was how the jetty was empty and that skiff had been there when he left out not a couple of hours before. His heart was pumping hard now and berthing his own boat, he took the steps as quickly as he could. In the yard, he could see a light at the kitchen window but he ignored that and raced to the workshop instead. It was empty. No Willow and no yellow oilskin. He stood there for a moment not quite sure what to do but she was gone all right and with the boat gone too that could only mean one thing.

Pious shuddered at the thought. He was as good on the water as anybody and he would not attempt to cross the shoals in a storm like this. He had to do something and quick. Running back across the yard he burst into the kitchen where he found John Q and his grandma sitting at the table with Noble Landry.

'Pious,' John Q stared at him. 'What's up?'

'Willow,' Pious blurted, he was looking at Noble, not quite understanding why he should be there. 'She ain't where she's supposed to be at. I think she done took off.'

'Took off for where?' John Q was on his feet.

'Half-Mile-Island I guess.'

Wide-eyed, John Q gawped. 'Willow's out in a boat? You're kidding me, Pious, right?'

Pious shook his head. He told them what had happened, how Willow had snuck into her great-grandpa's study and how she had hidden under the bed. He told them what she had overheard and how she had spoken to him right after. He told them how she had wanted to make the crossing and how he had brought her here and told her to hole up in the workshop instead. Only the workshop was empty and Grandma Q's skiff was gone from where it had been tied up.

Grandma Q looked up at him from where she was sitting at the table. Brows knit; she bunched her eyes at the corners.

'Grandma, we have to go look for her.' John Q rested his fists on the table. 'She'll be downriver or in the bay already. If we hurry we might get to her before she reaches The Dividing.'

'In this weather?' his grandmother looked doubtful.

'We have to try. We can't leave her out there in a boat.'

'Mrs Q, it's not storming as bad as it was,' Pious told her. 'I got up here real quick and that river ain't as high as she was.'

Still the old woman looked uncertain. 'Figure even if I forbid you you'll go just the same.'

John Q did not say anything.

'All right then, but for heaven's sake be careful. And Pious,' she lifted a bony finger, 'you-all run the boat.'

Pious dived for the door once more but John Q checked him. He went to his room and when he came back he was carrying the Winchester rifle. He looked at his grandma and she looked at him with one eyebrow hooked in an arch.

'I know I ain't fifteen here for another couple of weeks but after what Pious just said I figure Morgan J could do about anything.'

Still she looked at him.

'Grandma, you wouldn't have given me this rifle if you didn't think I knew how to use it.'

'I know that,' she said, 'but there's using it and there's using it.'

'Mrs Q,' Noble laid a hand on her arm. 'He's right about Morgan J.'

His grandmother seemed to think for a moment more. 'All right then,' she said. 'Take the gun but you be careful, you hear?'

They turned to go then Pious remembered why he had come in the first place. 'Mrs Quarrie,' he said, 'ma'am there's something else I got to tell you. Before I come on upriver just now I helped my mama with Mr Barra. Done lifted him out of his bed on account of she had to fix it up. Ma'am, he spoke to me, there was something I heard him say.'

'Spoke to you,' John Q peered from the doorway. 'Willow told me how he couldn't talk.'

'He can't,' Pious said. 'But I heard him just the same.'

'Heard what?' the old woman asked.

'You ma'am; 'your name, I heard him speak it to me.'

They took off up the yard with John Q carrying the rifle: 'Pious,' he said, 'why would that old man whisper to you about my grandma?'

'Beats me, but Miss Willow said how he was trying to tell her something only she never figured out what it was. I ain't deaf, John Q. I know what it is he said.'

Down at the landing they jumped in the boat and cast off and Pious told John Q to sit in the prow. 'Hold tight and don't be standing up again like you did the last time.'

Finding a spare oilskin under the seat John Q wrapped the Winchester in it. 'Don't worry about me,' he called. 'You just keep her pointed.'

Back at the house Noble was still in the kitchen. 'Mrs Q,' he said, 'I done set here too long. Morgan J will be looking for me and I know Chase is going to come down on me like I don't know what.' He sighed then wearily. 'Ma'am, I figure at least I got a clear conscience now I talked to you but that's all I got. If it's all right with you I'll just cut along.'

'No sir,' she said. 'It's not all right with me. Fact is, Noble; I ain't exactly sure where you can cut along to right now.' She gesticulated with the flat of her hand. 'You go back to that railroad car - what's going to happen?' She let him think about that then she said. 'You set there telling me how your life turned out and how it's been with your brother and all but before this night is done I figure things could get a whole lot worse for you or they could get a mite better.'

Sitting back with a fist bunched Noble drew in his brows. 'A mite better,' he said. 'How'd you figure that?'

With a knowing look the old woman smiled then. 'What you told me just now, I figure you ought to be telling it to somebody else.'

Noble looked horrified. 'You mean the sheriff?'

'That's exactly who I mean. If Morgan J really is trying to kill Cassie Flood and her daughter then he has to be stopped. Not only that, it's time Peyton and Chase got what's coming.'

'Mrs Q, I ain't sure I want to talk to....'

'Noble, I'm not sure you've got a choice.' She gripped his hand now. 'You don't have the codicil on account of I got it and I know you ain't going to try and take it from me. Right now the only choice you got is to light out of here and keep on going, either that or talk to the sheriff.' She got to her feet. 'I figure on you doing the latter because that's the right thing to do and in my experience you do the right thing and life will come around for you some. It's like that, Noble; what goes around comes around no matter what folk say.'

For a moment he thought about that.

'Now, listen to me,' she said, 'right about now Morgan J will be sniffing round that railroad car which means it's only Mama Sox up at Spanish Bluff.' Getting up from the table she went to the dresser and fetched a key tied to a length of string. 'In the garage there's a twenty year old Model T Ford. I want you to get her started and then I want you to drive me on up to the house.'

Bug-eyed, Noble peered at her.

'You can drive an automobile, can't you?'

'Yes ma'am, I can.'

'So go ahead.' She handed him the key. 'I'll get some clothes on while you see if you can't crank that handle.'

———

Morgan J pulled the Cadillac up to the empty lot and switched the head-lights off. There was a glow coming from the Pullman and for a moment he just sat there and considered it. Then he cast his eye across the two other railroad cars lying on their sides along with the wrecked automobiles.

He stood in the rain where it seemed to have slackened if only a little. Looking up at the sky he thought about how the call from Noble Landry had come too late and Chase had already been let loose. It could not be helped, it would mean there was only the daughter to deal with and despite the fact that he had the paperwork he was better off rid of them both. The way Chase would make it look Cassie would've wrecked on the highway and as far as her daughter was concerned he would figure that out later on. As soon as he was finished with Noble Landry he planned to go back to the house and sit down with his father. He would light a cigar, put a match to that codicil and while it burned in the ashtray he'd have the old man watch.

Tramping across the pot-holed lot, he picked his way around the fire stones where some kind of makeshift tripod was set. He glanced back up the deserted street towards the square but nobody was about.

'Noble,' he called. 'It's Morgan Barra. Come on out.'

There was no answer and, cursing under his breath, he made his way to the step. 'Noble,' he called again. 'For Christ's sake get out here and get this done.'

Still there was no answer.

'I have your money. I got your cash right here with me.'

No reply again so Morgan J climbed up. There was no door on the railroad car and he stepped inside being careful to avoid a rusty looking hinge that was sticking out.

The smell hit him, the stench of the place; it was old and damp and filthy. There were only two seats still fixed to the floor and apart from the table set between them they were the only furnishings. A hurricane lamp was burning on that table and it hissed and fizzed as though it was about to putter out. 'Noble,' he said, 'where the hell are you at?' He paused at the table and picking up the Mason jar, he inspected the dregs in the bottom. Beyond the two seats was an old tick of a mattress with a filthy rag thrown across it.

'He ain't around then, huh?'

Morgan J started as the voice seemed to leap from behind him.

Spinning round he saw Shoofly standing in the doorway. He looked unnervingly dapper with his hat hooked over one eye and a top coat draped across his shoulders.

'What you doing in a joint like this?' Shoofly asked him. 'I seen the fella they got living here and he don't look like your kind of company.'

Morgan J stared at him suddenly aware of his pulse. 'What're you doing here, Shoofly?'

'Me, I'm just moseying around; what you doing though, that's the question?'

Morgan J sighed then wearily. 'If you must know I'm looking for some papers, a codicil actually. Do you know what that is?'

'Sure I know what it is.'

Morgan J gestured. 'My father's will, there's an amendment and Noble Landry's got the paperwork only he's not here to meet me like he said.'

Slowly Shoofly nodded. 'He done cut you off then did he, the old man; turned out just like I thought.' He paused for a moment then added. 'So I'm thinking where does that leave the two of us exactly?'

'It leaves us right where we were before.' Again Morgan J gestured. 'The old man's dying, Shoofly; sicker than a dog with distemper and this is only temporary.' He took another look around the railroad car. 'Noble Landry has the papers and he's going to hand them over to me. Once I have them I will burn them. That means everything goes back to how it was and that means the entire estate is mine and that's a hell of a lot more than the fifty-thousand dollars I owe you.'

'I tell you what,' Shoofly suggested. 'I'd like to see you get a-hold of those papers. I'd like to see how you got them on account of I'd like to know they been burned already and that I don't have to kill you.' He turned his nose up at the stench. 'But it stinks worse than a sewer in here and it's raining out. I got me an automobile parked up the block. Rather than wait in this rat-hole why don't you come on back?'

'That's all right,' Morgan J told him. 'I got my own car.'

Shoofly nodded. 'I know you do, I seen her - the Cadillac.' Smiling coldly he gestured towards the doorway. 'Even so I'd like for you to set with me. Actually, now I come to think of it - I insist.'

———

TWENTY

John Q felt the wind hit hard as the mouth of the river opened up. They were almost into the bay now, the sky did not seem so dark and he could see the fullness of the channel where waves crested in flinted flakes.

'See if you can spot the boat,' Pious called to him.

'Doing that already,' John Q called back, 'but she's pretty dark out there and all I can see is the kind of water going to put us on the beach.'

Hunkering down in the prow, he looked back as Pious twisted the throttle grip. The bows came up and they chopped into the waves and the oilskin hood tightened around his face.

'Can't imagine she'd have tried to do this,' he yelled. 'Willow ain't stupid, Pious: maybe she went upriver.'

'What's upriver?' his friend called back. 'Miller's Town and Rutherford, there ain't nothing for her upriver. I talked to her, John Q and all she could go on about was crossing to the island.' With his free hand he gestured. 'Told me how she could hide out, said how it's the one place Morgan J wouldn't be able to find her.'

'You figure he'll be coming then, do you?' John Q shouted back.

Pious nodded to the oilskin wrapped around the rifle. 'You telling me you don't?'

The rain was falling hard and fast. They were into the early hours now and above their heads there was no break in the clouds whatever. Pious did his best to keep the prow pointed into the wind and they were jogging, riding waves that shook the boat and sometimes washed right over.

The waves left water in the bottom of the boat and salt to scatter their faces. When he wasn't baling, John Q had one eye on making sure his gun stayed dry and the other on the sea ahead. He could feel a pulse at his temple, he could feel his heart in his chest and his mouth was drier than when he'd woken up in that Pullman. He stared into the darkness, trying to see beyond the proximity of the swell. But it was impossible, so dark and they were so low down in such a small boat he couldn't see anything but the waves that were threatening to swamp them.

They were coming up on where the tides reversed and in this weather it was crazy. Pious was half-sitting, half-standing; gripping the tiller and trying to keep the boat from capsizing. Up ahead the waves smashed into one another as they carried the breadth of the sandbars.

'Hold on,' Pious yelled. 'This is where she gets antsy.'

It was touch and go as the boat wallowed deep in the troughs before scaling the heights as the sea seemed to boil all around them. More than once John Q felt the sandbars grate on the hull as Pious fought to stop them being grounded. He felt helpless, nothing he could do but hold on and yell out words of encouragement.

He had no idea how Pious managed it but somehow he got them through and as they hit the ocean proper John Q could only nod his head in admiration. But only for a moment; they had beaten the threat from the tides maybe but there were plenty of other threats still facing them.

'Hey bud,' Pious shouted. 'I reckon if Miss Willow made it this far she wouldn't try and cross bull shark bay, she'd make for the Orange Blossom River and come on through the marsh at the Jabberwock. I figure it's easier in there and that's where I'm going to take us.'

'You're the captain,' John Q called to him. 'Got to tell you, bud, I'm with you on not messing with bull sharks. Ain't seen a bucking horse yet can work a man worse than what we got going on and I don't want to be swimming up thataway.'

'Yeah well, we ain't bucked off just yet.' Pious smiled broadly. 'Hang on. She'll be quieter when we're in the marshes.'

He was right, as soon as they were into the arms of the muddy maze the wind seemed to drop right off although the rain still fell on them fearfully. For half an hour they ran the Jabberwock, switchbacking through the channels before once again they were in open water.

There was something up ahead now, something ominous. They both saw it and John Q was on his feet rocking unsteadily in the bows with his blood running cold as he realized what it was. 'Yonder,' he yelled. 'Pious, there's a boat busted up on the rocks.'

———

A dozen miles west of Spanish Fork, Chase Landry pulled the prowl car into the turnout off the rain washed, dirt road highway.

In the back seat Willow's mother was getting anxious. 'Chase,' she said, 'for God's sake. We have to get back to Spanish Bluff. Mr Barra has to have his medication.'

Twisting around where he sat Chase looked back at her. 'Mrs Flood,' he said, 'those meds aren't going to do any good. I spoke to Morgan Junior and he told me how it was with the old man. He's done for, dying: his time is over.'

For a moment she just stared at him. 'You talked to Morgan J?'

'Yes I did and just this evening.' Taking his hat from his head he worked the brim between his fingers.

Next to him Peyton looked over the seat and he was smiling only the smile was not very friendly. 'You know something,' he said, 'for all the world back there you look just like your mother.'

Cassie could feel herself trembling. 'Never mind my mother, Peyton. Chase, will you get this car started?'

'Cassie,' Chase said. 'I'm getting tired of you giving orders. You don't give orders anymore. That ain't your place any longer.' Sadly he wagged his head at her. 'You don't know what's been happening do you? You have no idea what's gone down between Morgan J and his father.'

'What're you talking about?' Trembling now, Cassie stared at him.

'I'm talking about all the trouble the old man's been causing. On account of you and your daughter, what he told Morgan Junior.'

Still she stared at him. Outside the force of the storm had picked up and the car was rocking on its springs. 'What're you talking about?' she repeated.

'I'm talking about how he changed his will to favor you and your brat of a daughter. You didn't know about that now, did you?'

Dumbstruck, Cassie just sat there. With a slow smile Chase went on, his mouth a little slack at the corners.

'It was only this morning,' he said. 'Morgan J told us how the old man called him out to the patio up at the big house and told him he was leaving you every last cent of his fortune.'

Still Peyton was peering over the back of the seat. 'You really do look just like her,' he repeated, 'how she was that night. Remember how she looked, Chase, in Koontz bar when Morgan J wasn't going to take her home no matter how bad she was bitching?'

———

They were in the "Speakeasy" Willy Koontz had created in the basement of his cafe. With the Volstead Act just passed it was the only place where you could get a drink and Laurel was down there with Morgan Junior. They had come over to eat dinner because he insisted and she wanted to go back right after because her daughter was on her own and she didn't like to drink anyway.

But Morgan J did like to drink and he wasn't about to leave and Laurel had to be there to keep him sweet because all summer he had been hanging out on Half-Mile Island. He was hiding from people he owed money to and he spent his time moaning and fishing and knocking back illicit whiskey. Whenever he felt like it he threatened the islanders with eviction just like he had done every other time he had been over there. It was ten years since he first showed up and ten years later he was still making the same threats and it was only Laurel who had been able to placate him. She had done so then and she was doing it now but she was growing weary.

After dinner she tried to persuade him to drive straight back to the mooring but he told her it was too dark already and they were bound to get stuck on a sandbar. Laurel reminded him that she could navigate the shoals wearing a blindfold so the darkness wasn't anything they had to worry about. But he wasn't having any of it.

Koontz's was packed of course, and Morgan J was entertaining everybody including Peyton and Chase who made sure the place never got raided. He was telling stories about life on the boardwalk in Atlantic City; how he rubbed shoulders with gangsters like Dandy Nichols and they were all of them goggle-eyed listening.

'All kinds of deals go down,' Morgan J was saying, 'you even got coloreds up there running their own show and that ain't just the booze it's gambling and everything. I swear there ain't anything you want you can't get in Atlantic City.' Slipping an arm around Laurel's waist he drew her to him. 'I know all the best places and there's not a body anywhere who doesn't know Morgan Junior. Isn't that right, honey?'

Laurel did not say anything. She just sat there looking coldly at Peyton.

'I said, isn't that right, honey?' Morgan J repeated.

Still she didn't answer and with a shake of his head he turned his back on her.

For a moment Laurel sat there looking foolish then she patted him on the arm. 'Morgan, can we please go home now?'

'The hell we can,' he muttered, 'this party's just getting started.

'I want to go now. Can we please go back to the landing?'

Chase was looking over Morgan J's shoulder at her. 'You talking about the island; crossing those shoals in the dark?' He shook his head. 'Stick around, honey. This place is where it's at right now and nobody's going to disturb us.'

'But my daughter......'

'The girl is just fine,' Morgan J spoke without looking at her. 'For Christ' sake she's with that nigger woman looks after her, what the hell can happen?'

For a moment Laurel stared again at the back of his head then she slapped him across the ear.

The sound was so loud the barroom was suddenly silent. Morgan J almost tipped off his stool and Chase shifted uneasily. Peyton sat back looking at Laurel with his lips wet and eyes tight. Grabbing Laurel by the wrist Morgan J dragged her upstairs and out to the highway.

'What the hell do you think you're doing?' he demanded. 'You don't slap me. Jesus, woman, I'm Morgan Barra Junior.'

Ignoring him she walked across the road to where he had left the Ford. 'I'm going home,' she told him. 'Either you're driving me to the landing or I'm going to drive myself.'

Ear still raw, Morgan J stared after her. 'You're not driving that car. It isn't mine and you're not driving. You might be able to run a boat, hell there's not much to crash in to, but you don't know what you're doing in a vehicle. Woman, I swear every tree by the road's going to feel like it's jumping out on you.' His eyes darkened. 'I tell you what though, you make me drive and I will dump your ass at the landing and that'll be the last you see of me till I show up over there with the bailiff.'

'Show up with who you like.' Laurel told him, 'just take me back to the boat.'

He stood there with one hand lifted to his ear. 'I don't believe you,' he said: 'you hit me in front of everyone and then demand I take you home. I tell you, lady you are some kind of..........'

'JUST DO IT, WILL YOU?' She was screaming at him. 'Take me home for God's sake. I want to see my daughter.' She was in his face, fists bunched, spittle raking her lips. Grabbing the key from his hand, she fumbled at the dashboard but she had no idea what she was doing. Morgan J came up behind her. 'I swear to God,' he said. 'I ought to take a switch to you right where you're standing.'

Peyton appeared from the steps of the speakeasy behind them. 'Is everything all right, Mr Barra?' he called. 'Chase wanted to know if you needed anything.'

'Like a ride home?' Morgan scoffed. 'I'm fine, Peyton: everything is peachy.'

'Maybe you ought to let one of us take you-all back to the landing. Wouldn't want you to be wrecking; not out there, folk might think you'd been drinking. What with your father being who he is and all where would that leave the department?'

'To hell with my father, Peyton; and to hell with the sheriff's department.' Shunting Laurel into the passenger seat, Morgan J fitted the key in the dashboard then shifted the spark lever under the steering wheel to advance and opened the throttle a fraction. Engine primed he walked around the front.

'Can't get used to this damn vehicle,' he muttered. 'It's hardly a Cadillac is it?' Grabbing the starter handle with his left hand he gripped the fender for support with his right and cranked one half turn. The engine fired and he walked around to the driver's side.

Behind the wheel, he pulled away from the kerb and squinted sideways at Laurel.

'Comfy are you?' he asked her. 'You damn well ought to be.'

In high gear he drove at twenty miles an hour. When they hit the River Road he opened the accelerator as far as it would go and the speed crept up to forty.

'You're going too fast,' Laurel warned him. 'Morgan J, you need to slow down.'

He laughed at her. 'You're the one wanted to go.'

They were into the thickest trees, the road narrow where the branches were overhanging and he was taking the bends too quickly. Looking over his shoulder he could see lights coming up behind now. They stayed a little way back and when he slowed they did, when he sped up they sped up and he figured it was Peyton shadowing them. Chase must have sent him to make sure they made it to the landing. That was fine because he was pretty loaded right now but he could relax knowing he had a cop riding shotgun.

Plucking a cigar from his pocket he tried to light it but the match kept blowing out. No roof on the Ford, the night full of stars; a coughing fit took him, his eyes watered and for a moment his vision was blurred. The road had narrowed to nothing and before he realised what was happening they were into the bend at Bluff Bridge and below them the whirlpool was boiling.

The steering wheel was spinning under his hand; the back end fishtailing badly. They slammed into a tree and Morgan J was thrown from the car. He was in the dirt and rolling hard; he hit his head but did not black out. He lay on his side looking on in a kind of stupor.

He could see the car thrashing through the scrub. He could see it skidding between the skinny trunks of trees. It upended, obliterating the front fender and buckling the hood. He could see Laurel still in the passenger's seat. She was screaming. He could hear her voice above the bellow of the water and for a split second he saw her being tossed around like a rag doll, her hair translucent in the moonlight. Then the car disappeared and he could hear it shuddering over rocks, metallic grunts, the sound of glass shattering, he could hear the tearing of metal as the body opened up. Above it all he could hear the water and above the water the sound of her voice still screaming.

For a long time afterwards he lay by the side of the road. His head ached: he felt bile in his throat and he threw up. Wiping his mouth he thought he saw a point of light shining from further down the highway. A minute or so later he heard the crunch of boots and someone had a flashlight in his face.
'Mr Barra,' he heard his name being called. 'Mr Barra, are you all right?'

Peyton Skipwith: dumbly, Morgan J looked up at him. Then Peyton had him on his feet, one arm about his shoulders he was supporting his weight. He got him to the bridge where he sat him down with his back to the stonework.

Leaning over the wall Peyton shone the flashlight into the depths. The Pit; that whirlpool there was no escaping, with so much water being compressed into such a small space it bellowed like a gun-shot bear.
'Saw what all happened and I got to tell you,' he said, dropping to his haunches. 'That automobile is gone and that woman is gone along with it.

There's no way she's going to get out of there and even if she was alive there's no way I could help her without getting sucked into that hellhole myself.' Falling silent, he seemed to take a moment to think. 'Mr Barra,' he went on finally. 'Chase done told me, Chase said to me that in a situation like this, when what's done is done and can't be undone, in a situation like this you have to keep your head. Do you hear me, Mr Barra? You have to keep your wits about you.'

He snaked his tongue across his lips. 'Fact is I heard what she said just now, how she was determined to go home no matter that Chase himself told her not to make the call.' His eyes were dark, his features pinched. 'I guess she'd been buying whatever it was she'd been drinking from some no-good shiner and I guess she was determined to drive no matter how liquored up she was. I guess you-all jumped in at the last minute after you saw how she was taking off with your vehicle. Spotted you myself just now as you come running out of the diner.' Gently he patted Morgan's cheek now. 'Did you hear me, Mr Barra? I saw you coming out of the diner.'

———

In the back seat of the prowl car Cassie could feel the heat of tears as they rolled on her cheeks.

Still Peyton leered at her. 'We were there, Mrs Flood; that night when your momma was out on his dollar. She didn't like to drink so much as I recollect but she could sure set down to dinner.'

Next to him Chase flared his nostrils. 'That's a fact,' he said. 'Morgan J might not have laid out hard cash dollars exactly but she was getting plenty for the favors she was offering.'

Trembling now Cassie stared between them. She knew what this was about. She knew why they had been driving the Rutherford road. They weren't looking for a fugitive they were there at the behest of Morgan Junior.

Wiping away her tears she spoke to Peyton. 'So Morgan J was driving the car that night and you lied to coroner.'

'Had to be done,' he told her.

'He lost control on the bridge.'

'Happens that way when it's whiskey people been drinking.' Peyton shrugged. 'I figure Morgan J can hold his liquor as well as anybody but most doctors will tell you how it dulls the senses. Road like that at night, the way the bridge sort of swings up on you. In a beat up old car like that there ain't no time to think and there wasn't any way he could've made it.'

Cassie sobbed now, she could not help herself and the tears just fell. Chase studied her in the rear view mirror.

'Crying ain't going to cut it,' he said. 'You might as well quit that because crying ain't going to make any difference.'

'Willow,' Cassie whispered. 'Where's my daughter?'

'Right now I can't tell you,' Chase said, 'but I figure the next time you see her it won't be this side of any horizon.' Opening the door he got out. 'Time to take some air, Mrs Flood: come ahead and get out of the car now.'

———

TWENTY-ONE

Noble got the Model T started and backed it out of the lean-to. By the time he was ready Grandma Q was dressed and waiting on the porch. He pulled around front and she came striding up the path still carrying the twelve-gauge shotgun.

'That piece there to keep an eye on me?' Noble asked her.

'No it isn't. Fact is I've decided I'm going to trust you, Noble. I figure if a few more people had done that down the years then things might have turned out different. Seems to me if you wanted to take off now was the time and you ain't done it so I don't believe you're going to. No sir,' she said, 'this shotgun isn't for you. It's along on account of how we might run into Morgan Junior.'

They drove east and old as it was, Noble seemed to be enjoying the vehicle. 'Can't tell you when I was last in an automobile; seen the back of a truck plenty these past six months but not the wheel of a motor car.'

'Man should drive every once in a while,' Grandma Q told him. 'Does him good I reckon.'

Noble nodded. 'Did you have an automobile when your husband was alive still?'

'No, we didn't. He was gone by nineteen and eighteen, this is the only one I ever owned and she's the twenty-seven model.'

'They say Henry Ford wanted everybody driving.' Noble gestured expansively. 'I guess there was a time when most folks had a horse and a wagon maybe, buckboard; something like that. I figure when he come along he reckoned everybody should have a car. Kindly like to have one myself one of these days, but I ain't sure that's going to happen.'

The old woman glanced sideways at him. 'You never can tell, Noble: folk have no idea how a thing's going to pan out and the way life is sometimes she can surprise you. What I always told my boy, the same I tell my grandson; good or bad, if you put yourself in the way of something then something just might happen.'

Driving out to the bluff they slowed at the gates to the house. There the gravel drive stretched between live oaks where great webs of Spanish moss shimmered in the rain soaked branches. This was as far as the road went; the end of the line; after that the land just drifted into the coast and that was all there was of America.

Noble pulled up outside the garage doors and the only lights they could see were in the kitchen. He was nervous, this was Morgan Junior's house and Noble did not want to face him.

'Mrs Quarrie,' he began. 'I know what we said and all but I figure I......'

'Don't figure on anything but staying right where you're at,' she told him. 'Now, I'm going in the house and I want you to wait here for me. If this is what I think it is then I'll be back soon enough because it might-could be we're driving.'

Leaving him alone she crossed the patio where the wind sculled the surface of the swimming pool. Through the kitchen window she could see Mama Sox resting an elbow on the table with her chin in a palm and her eyes closed tightly.

Grandma Q bustled in and Mama Sox was on her feet trying to make it look as if she had not been asleep. Her brows were knit and her gaze unfocused; she peered at the old woman as if she couldn't get her head around her being there.

'I'm here to see Mr Barra, Mama,' Grandma Q told her. 'I heard how he was sick.'

Mama Sox stared at her. She stared at the clock. 'Mrs Q, it's three o'clock in the morning.'

'Never mind what time it is. Where is Morgan Junior?'

The housekeeper shrugged. 'I ain't seen him since he went out. A while ago now that'd be I reckon.'

'Good, he won't be getting in my way then.'

Grandma Q walked up the passage to the hall and crossed beyond the staircase to the study. She knew this house, though she had been here only once and that was a long time ago.

'Mrs Q,' Mama Sox came scurrying up behind her, 'you can't go in the study. Mr Barra is sick and he'll be sleeping right now. I can't have you-all disturb him.'

'He's not sleeping.' Grandma Q looked over her shoulder. 'Go back to the kitchen, Mama; Mr Barra is waiting on me. He told your boy how he wanted to see me.'

'Pious?' Mama Sox gawped at her. 'How could he tell him that? Mr Barra, he can't talk anymore he's not able.'

'Well that's doctors for you. According to Pious he managed a whisper.' Grandma Q looked hard at her. 'Listen to me, this is important so go on and let me be.' Her eyes were sharp and without waiting for further protest she opened the study door.

It was very dark in the room, the only light drifting from the lamp by the bed where the angle of the shade shielded half of it. The door clicked to and she crossed the floor to where the old man looked up at her. One side of his face was frozen, the only hint of anything was in his eyes and as Grandma Q looked into them she thought she saw hope or something akin to it.

'Mr Barra, sir,' she said gently. 'It's Grandma Quarrie the midwife. Young Pious said how you wanted to see me.'

He could not say anything. He could not move. All he could do was look up at her.

'You always told me that if the time ever came you would let me know and I guess that time is now then.'

Still he peered at her. He blinked once and Grandma Q glanced across the room to the desk where an assortment of papers scattered the surface. 'I imagine the paperwork's in here somewhere and I guess they need to see it finally.'

He blinked again very slowly.

'Well I doubt I'm going to be able find it because knowing you, sir; you got it hid pretty well.' She got to her feet now. 'It doesn't matter. Leave it to me, Mr Barra. There's another way to do this and I got a car outside now waiting.'

———

Morgan J could not get away from Shoofly. For an hour they sat in his car watching the railroad but there was no sign of Noble Landry.

'Sure is taking his time,' Shoofly stated. 'Any which way you look at it the man be taking his time.' He paused for a moment then he spoke to the two goons up front. 'Figure we saw the sucker earlier, shabby looking fella come into the hotel lobby just after I got done talking on the telephone.'

Next to him Morgan J was restless. 'Look, Shoofly,' he said, 'this is all well and good but I really have to get back now.'

'Get back to what?' Shoofly turned to him. 'If this guy has the papers then he's who you need to be talking to and you don't need to be getting back to no place.'

It was a fact and there was nothing Morgan J could say to counter it. He worked a palm across the sweat that was lining his brow.

'You really are enjoying this aren't you,' he said. 'I mean how often is it you get to put this kind of hurt on a man like me.'

'This kind of hurt?' Shoofly wagged his head. 'This ain't hurt, Morgan J: you want to see me put the hurt on somebody just wait till I know how you ain't going to pay me.'

'Shoofly, of course I'm going to pay you.' Morgan J tried to smile now but he was sweating profusely. 'If you didn't believe that then why buy the debt from Dandy Nicholls in the first place?'

Shoofly smiled then and lightly patted Morgan J on the knee. 'Fact is Dandy didn't think you would pay. He figured he was going to have to kill you and be done with it and it crossed his mind about how he might enjoy that. But then he started thinking of what-all it might bring down on him politically. In the end I guess that with his kind of ambitions it wasn't something he could have people be suggesting. He offered your ass at seventy cents on the dollar and that's a pretty good deal right there. Guess it shows just how keen he was to be shut of you.'

Casually now he gestured. 'Fact is, I got no compunction about killing you, none whatever. Don't matter to me if you're a Barra or a McElroy or the King of England, money owed is money owed and if it ain't paid there has to be consequences.' He let that sentence hang between them for a moment then reaching across he opened the other door. 'But of course I'd rather that you pay me, Morgan J and taking account of the vig that's close to sixty thousand dollars. Find this fella you got to find and do what it is you got to do.' His eyes were dull as coal now. 'You don't and I have to come visit with you again I promise I'll make it painful and I promise I'll make it slow.'

The boat was Grandma Q's all right, wrecked on the rocks on the outer lip of the lagoon. Pious did his best to come alongside but he could not get close, it was all he could do to negotiate the passage where the waves and the wind were menacing.

They looked on in silence the two of them. The little craft had all but disintegrated; the engine gone, hull smashed. Pious had tears building.

'I told her not to do it,' he uttered finally, 'told her to hold up in that workshop till we could figure out what to do.' He shook his head. He pressed fingers into his eyes to try and stop tears falling. 'Should've knowed she wasn't going to listen, should have seen that with her right off.'

'Pious, it ain't your fault.' John Q was unable to drag his gaze from where the shattered boat was pinned. He had that same ache in his chest from before only now it hurt with a vengeance. 'You did what you could and it ain't your fault. Come on,' he said. 'We ain't out of this ourselves yet are we.' He pointed into the distance. 'What d'you reckon, can we make it to the beach there yonder?'

Pious tightened his grip once more on the throttle. Concentrating hard, he rode the Shark's Teeth with the swell, keeping the bows straight and cutting right through the middle of the channel. After that they wallowed between waves momentarily but they were in slack water. From there it was a matter of running in and tying up at the ancient jetty.

John Q jumped out and secured the bowline. When the stern was tied he grabbed the oilskin wrap and his rifle. The wind had lessened a fraction and the rain was no longer coming down quite so fiercely.

'Pious,' he peered into his friend's face through the darkness. 'It ain't raining like it was but we're pretty much soaked and I figure we need to get us some shelter.'

Together they made their way up the beach and when they got to the terraces Pious gestured. 'Reckon my mama's old place be as good as any.'

John Q nodded. Despite the oilskins they were shivering and Pious' teeth had started to chatter. John Q gazed across the lagoon to the rocks where the wreck of his grandma's boat was no longer visible.

'Can't believe we made it,' he said. 'No wonder they call her The Dividing; figure a stretch like that kind of separates the dead from the living.'

Pious glanced at him and John Q glanced back and, with a shake of his head, he looked away. He had opened his mouth and spoken the words before he really thought about what he was saying. Willow in that tiny vessel at the mercy of the sea, he tried not to think about how frightened she would've been and he prayed she had drowned and that no bull shark had come anywhere near her. He bit his lip. He shook his head. He looked again at Pious.

'You liked her whole hell of a lot, didn't you?' Pious peered from under his hood. 'Could see it the first time you laid eyes on her.'

'By the side of the road there with that flat tire.' Features taut now, John Q nodded.

'Was barely a couple of days back, John Q; feels like a hell of a lot longer.'

'Yeah it does.' John Q puckered his gaze to the rain. 'Can't think about that now though, figure we're going to need to get a fire going so we can get these clothes dry or we could be in some kind of trouble. You ever hear of hypothermia?'

'Hypo –what?'

'Too much cold: too much rain; it's where the temperature of your body gets too low and can't get back to normal. My uncle told me if that happens, you fall into a sleep you don't wake up from. We got to get our clothes dry, bud. You got any matches do you?'

Pious gazed the length of the beach: 'Could be some in the boat maybe.'

John Q watched as he ran all the way back to the mooring. He stood in the trees with the wind blowing the weight of the rain across him. Again he thought about that boat and again he thought about Willow and he could see her outside the drugstore breaking a Popsicle with her mother. He could see her with her finger over the hole in that inner tube and he could feel her there beside him. John Q had never been one for crying but he was close now and he blinked hard to keep the tears at bay.

A few minutes later Pious was back with an oilskin bag he had taken from the water-tight locker in the boat. 'Matches,' he said, 'and a flare gun I guess they kept for emergencies.'

Together they trotted the length of the terrace, Pious with the oilskin bag and John Q with his rifle. They got to the last cabin and Pious pushed open the door. He stopped dead and it was so dark John Q didn't notice and clattered right into him. Looking over his friend's shoulder he saw a shadow on the floor and for a moment he thought of what Willow had told them about bears crossing from the mainland.

They stood there in absolute silence. Then slowly Pious opened the bag and took out the matches. Striking one he lifted it above his head. John Q looked where he did and there was Willow lying asleep on the floor.

———

TWENTY-TWO

In the clearing her mother got out of the prowl car. Ducking her head she rested one hand on the back of the driver's seat where Chase was at the door. She could see his potbelly sagging over his belt. She could see his gun slung low on his hip. Peyton was on the other side where the wind was whipping through the trees and Cassie lunged with her head down and butted Chase right in the sternum. She heard him gasp; saw him clutch his middle then he staggered back into the door. Cassie did not stop moving. She was past him, the momentum carrying her at a half-crouch, she disappeared into the darkness.

She heard Peyton yell out. She waited for the sound of a gunshot but none came and then she doubted they would want to shoot her anyway. They would try to make it look like an accident, make it seem as if she had left her car and continued on foot and had come to grief in the trees.

She still had hold of the paper sack containing the blood thinning drugs for her grandpa. Somehow she hadn't dropped it when she butted Chase and she clutched it to her as she ducked beneath the branches. They were coming. She saw the wash from their torches fall across the woodland to her left then it panned right suddenly and covered her in a translucent curtain.

She had to get away from that flashlight. She had to hide. There were two of them and they had weapons and they were faster on foot than she was. She wore shoes with heels and they were no good in the woodland. Ducking into a deeper copse the trees grew close all around her. She stood there unable to see anything. The sharpened points of branches were dragging at her hair, scraping her face; they threatened to put her eyes out. Moving again she had to duck lower and lower to avoid them, one hand shading her eyes she was conscious of the tightness of her breath, the way she was laboring with sudden exertion.

Again the beam from a flashlight spread across the ground right in front of her and she shrank into the shadows. She spotted a mound of earth, a rock covered in moss and lichen and she ducked down in the cover behind it.

She sat there with her back to the wet rock and her breath coming in short gasps and all the time she could hear those deputies getting closer. She heard them talking, she heard them muttering; she heard their curses. They would spot this rock soon enough and figure out it was where she was hiding. She had to move again and quickly. Taking off her shoes she held them in one hand and the paper sack in the other while she crawled on her knees and elbows.

———

The match gave out, Pious struck another and John Q stared at Willow. Her eyes were open now and she looked up and she was shivering. Her teeth were chattering. He could see how her clothes were as soaking wet as theirs were.

'We thought you were dead,' his voice was not much more than a whisper. It was as if he did not believe she was there. 'Pious saw the boat gone and we came out to find you.' He gestured a little hopelessly. 'The rocks; my grandma's boat, Willow, we saw her all smashed to pieces.'

Willow blinked hard and the tears that laced her eyes glimmered in the half-light. The second match burned out and Pious struck a third.

'I'm sorry,' Willow said. 'I didn't mean to wreck your grandma's boat. I....'

'Don't worry about the boat.' John Q dropped to one knee beside her. 'Who cares about the boat, we thought you were dead: me and Pious thought you-all were drowned.'

Throwing her arms around his neck she hugged him. He wasn't expecting it. Maybe she wasn't but she was in his arms now and he held her.

'The engine died. I had no way of steering the boat.' She was sobbing. 'A wave hit and I was in the sea. The oilskin, I thought it was going to drag me under.'

Still John Q held her. He could feel how cold she was, how wet her clothes were and just how much she was shivering. He looked up at Pious as the new match guttered and died now. 'Pious,' he said. 'We got to get us a fire going.'

Pious spoke through the darkness. 'Guess we got a stove in back that ought to still be working; it ain't but a pot belly with a length of pipe up through the roof but unless some bird nested in her she ought to still clear smoke. Fetch us some wood, figure we can get her burning.'

Taking another match he struck it and peered at Willow. 'Miss Willow,' he said. 'I done told you not to try and cross The Dividing.'

Willow looked sheepish. 'I know you did and I should've listened, but I almost made it.'

'Almost ain't enough, good job you been coming here your whole life, good job you know how to be swimming when that tide is rolling.' The match burned out and he dropped it then took another. Striking that he indicated the cast iron stove and John Q went to work on it.

It was opened by a lid at the top but it was sealed fast and he had to prise it up with the blade of his clasp knife. Inside it was thick with old spiders' webs and he scraped them clear and used his knife on a patch of ancient ash that had hardened to a paste in the base.

'All right, Pious,' he said when he was finished, 'if that stack don't smoke us out this ought to work. Need to get us some dry wood though like you said; only it's pretty darn wet out there.'

'Yeah it is,' Pious peered through the window, 'but I figure there's plenty old chairs and whatnot in the other huts. Come on; let's see what we can come up with.'

Leaving Willow, they stepped back into the storm. They broke the door on the next hut where it was almost off its hinges anyway and inside they found bits of old table and broken chairs. The roof had clearly been leaking but only in patches and the timber seemed dry enough. Between them they broke it up by stamping on it and carried it across the clearing.

Back in Pious' hut they fed the stove and then Pious struck another match and put it to the smallest flakes of wood. They did not seem to want to burn though, and he had to coax them by blowing gently. Finally a couple caught and an orange flame fluted. John Q watched him work. Willow watched him and John Q cocked an eyebrow where her clothes were sticking to her.

'Willow,' he said. 'Only way to get warm is to get out of your clothes. Only way they're going to dry is if you lay them out by the fire. Same goes for me and Pious.'

Uncertainly now she peered at him.

'I ain't talking naked,' he told her. 'I guess we can set in our underwear, but if we're going to get warm we have to lay out our top clothes at least so they can dry properly.'

Without a word Willow was on her feet stepping into the shadows away from the glow of the stove. She started to unbutton her blouse. John Q tugged off first one boot and then the other and set them side by side. He took off his jeans and his shirt and next to him Pious stripped down to his shorts. They draped their wet clothes as best they could and then sat on the floor in a semi-circle. In the distance they could hear the rumble of thunder and moments later the little room was lit by a flash of sheet lighting. Three of them almost naked, they looked at one another and the light went out and the thunder passed above them.

It was getting warmer and they were no longer shivering. 'Pious,' John Q said, 'I have to tell you, bud; if it wasn't for you piloting that skiff like that none of us would even be set here.'

'Willow would,' Pious corrected him. 'She made it without the fact her boat capsized, got clear across the water.'

'Yeah she did, but without us being here now she'd be freezing cold and soaking wet and I doubt she'd have gotten through till morning.'

———

Morgan J drove back to Spanish Bluff. He drove quickly, still smarting from the way Noble had double-crossed him. He had no codicil and he had no idea where Willow was, the only saving grace was that by now Chase and Peyton should have come across her mother.

Close to the house he passed an old Model T coming the other way and he was reminded of that night when he and Laurel had been in the speakeasy. It was a long time ago now and since then he had been trying to put his plans for Half-Mile Island into action and yet it remained as those squatters had left it.

Back at the house he left the car on the driveway and went in through the kitchen where Mama Sox was asleep at the table. The slamming of the door woke her and she sat up bleary-eyed and almost fell over in her rush to get to her feet.

'Mama,' Morgan J said. 'Has anybody telephoned?'

Mama looked up at him, blinking hard with tiredness. 'No sir,' she said. 'Nobody telephoned.'

He studied her now with his head tilted. 'You were asleep, how would you know if they did?'

'I can hear the telephone, Mr Morgan; even if I'm sleeping.' She looked at the clock on the wall. 'And where is it you been till four o'clock in the morning?'

'Where I've been isn't any of your business.'

'No sir. That's right, of course it ain't. I shouldn't be asking.'

Still he looked at her. 'You're sure you'd have heard the phone?'

'Mr Morgan, that phone got a ringer on it loud enough to wake the dead never mind no dozing housekeeper.'

He half-smiled at that despite himself. He worked a hand across his forehead.

'You-all want me to make you some coffee?' Mama asked him

'No,' he said. 'I don't want you to make coffee. What I want is a shot of bourbon.'

Mama Sox sat him down at the oak table and fetched a tumbler from the cupboard and a bottle of Jim Beam from the living room. Unscrewing the cap she tipped in a couple of fingers and he nodded for her to add a couple more.

'You look beat,' she told him. 'What's going on, Mr Morgan, what-all is happening?'

Morgan J inspected his glass. 'Go ahead and pour yourself one.'

'No sir, thank you. Saw what it did to my husband.' She sat down on the other side of the table. 'So what's going on, sir? Just an hour past I had Grandma Q in here wanting to see your daddy.'

Morgan J swallowed whiskey and set the glass down on the table. 'Who's Grandma Q?' he asked.

'Mrs Quarrie what lives on Riverview Road.'

'Don't know her. What was she doing here?'

'She was the midwife way back when, used to deliver the babies born on Half-Mile Island.'

'Is that a fact?' Again Morgan J sipped whiskey. 'What was she doing here?'

Mama Sox lifted her shoulders. 'Well sir, she done told me Mr Barra said to my boy how he wanted and all to see her.'

Morgan J paused with the glass almost to his lips but not quite. He stared at her. 'My father asked to see her? How can that be, Mama; my father can't talk.'

'That's what I told Grandma Q. I said to her how he'd had a stroke and all, how his brain was affected. She told me Pious said he wanted to see her.'

'What the hell was your son doing with my father?' His tone was terse now and across the table Mama sat more upright.

'He was helping me get his bed made up for the night,' she told him. 'You weren't here to do it. There still ain't no sign of Mrs Flood being back from the hospital and I can't lift that man on my own.'

'Cassie's not made it back yet?' Swallowing the rest of his drink Morgan J reached for the bottle.

'No sir, I ain't seen hide nor hair of her since she took off and all to get that medicine.'

'Well, it's blowing fit to bust out there,' Morgan J glanced towards the darkened window. 'Maybe she had an accident.'

Looking at him wide-eyed, the housekeeper made the sign of the cross then she kissed the tips of her fingers.

———

Cassie picked her way through the trees. The time had slipped by and they hadn't stopped searching but still they hadn't found her. In another hour or so the night would be over. She still had hold of her shoes though her nylons were torn to shreds, her skirt hemmed and her blouse ripped in the sleeve. Her nerves were as frayed as her clothes but so far she had managed to keep ahead of the two deputies and all she could think about was her great-grandpa having changed his will so she and Willow would inherit everything. That's what Chase had said. His only son disinherited; even with how they felt about each other that didn't add up. Morgan was a fair man, an honest man, a man who did right by everyone. Why would he cut his only son from his estate in favor of a squatter's child he'd adopted?

She had no idea but she also knew she could not afford to worry about it now. She needed all her wits about her just to stay alive. She could hear them hunting, searching; she could see the pale wash from their flashlights as it swept the tree trunks. It occurred to her that she had probably been leading them miles away from their prowl car and if she could just figure out where it was, if she could somehow get back to it, the keys were most likely still in the ignition. But she had no idea which direction to go; she had no idea which direction she had come from. She had been running any which-way and for all she knew she had been going around in circles.

All at once the light that had been distant a moment before, came peeling towards her and she dropped to the forest floor. She lay there trembling as the beam seemed to rush right across her. The wind had dropped and she lay where she was as one of the deputies walked so close he almost trod on her. She was silent, a huddle among the ferns and fallen leaves; half covered in mud where the rain had churned up the forest floor.

She heard a mutter, a grunt, a curse. She saw light drift and briefly she picked out the clearing where they had stopped and then she spotted the prowl car. It was only for an instant but her heart began to thump as she realised she had not taken them miles away after all.

Now she lay with her head pounding as she tried to work out what to do. Half-raised on an elbow she watched where the wash from the closest flashlight cast across every rock and root, every fallen branch and every nook and cranny. She lay flat once more as it carried the base of the trees and she brought her knees to her chest and tucked her head in tightly. For a second time the light passed right across her. Away it went and she heard the sound of retreating footfall. But still she lay there. How long before they gave up the search? How long before they figured out that they ought to wait until it was morning?

On her feet again, she picked her way carefully where she could make out the shadows of the branches. She made her way through them, trying to stay quiet then the trees cleared and she was on a path and she began to run towards the turnout where Chase had pulled off the highway. She ran until she got to the clearing and there was the car and she ducked down where the driver's door was still open. To her horror a shout lifted from further up the trail. They must've heard her, seen her and looking back she could see the flashlights bobbing her way. She was behind the wheel though and there was the key as she had thought, still fixed in the ignition.

Trembling, she turned the key and slammed the door and fumbled for the starter. In the dark she could not find it, a button under the wheel on the left, finally she got to it and the engine fired then she hit the headlights. She saw Peyton Skipwith running through the trees. He was reaching for his pistol but Cassie was hauling on the wheel and she would not allow him to shoot her.

Determined to stop her he jumped out in front of the car. She could not avoid him. Caught in the light from the headlamps she saw how she clipped him, heard the sickening thud and watched his eyes peel back in horror. She heard gun shots ring out then but none found their mark and she was free of the clearing and fishtailing down the highway.

———

John Q woke to what seemed a sudden stillness. It was getting light outside and the storm had finally abated. He was lying next to the stove where the embers from last night were just about still burning and all he wore were his shorts. Next to him Pious lay asleep and he too wore only his shorts. On the other side of the stove Willow was sound asleep still and for a long moment John Q stared at her. She looked peaceful; content, happy almost; her knees curled up with traces of sand still scattering her skin.

As quietly as he could John Q gathered up his clothes where he had laid them out and they were dry now and he tucked them under his arm. Outside, he propped the Winchester against a tree and put the clothes on. Then he walked the length of the terrace and beyond the lagoon all seemed calm across The Dividing. There was no wind now, only a few wisps of cloud; the storm had passed and no doubt it was battering the world further north. From where he stood he could see the mouth of the river and the headland at Spanish Bluff. He felt strangely peaceful and when he thought of how Willow had made it, how he and Pious had found her, he could feel tears in his eyes and silently he let them tumble.

———

TWENTY-THREE

Morgan J stood on the lip of the bluff overlooking the Atlantic Ocean. He could see the shoals where only thin ripples were breaking on the sandbars now and all looked calm in open water. Through his binoculars he could pinpoint the mouth of the Orange Blossom River and the marshes; the lagoon where the squatters used to bathe. He could see the beachhead and the trees that shrouded the huts and there a narrow wisp of woodsmoke was rising.

He could not be sure it was smoke; so often after a storm like the one just passed mist would drift above the trees in what looked like tendrils of smoke only it was water vapor. What he witnessed now might just be residue from the storm but then it might be a wisp of woodsmoke.

Lowering the binoculars, he walked back to the house and slowly, deliberately, he climbed the stairs to his bedroom. From the nightstand drawer beside the bed he took a velvet case that covered a wooden box which seemed to weigh heavily when he lifted it. For a second or so he just had it there in both hands then he laid it down on the bed. It was fitted with a brass clip at the front and two brass hinges at the back and the name "Samuel Colt" was burned into the top of the lid. Inside it was fitted with a series of velvet-lined compartments and broken open among them were the components of a pistol.

Casting the box aside, Morgan J assembled the gun. An automatic; slipping home the magazine the metallic clicks almost made him start and when he caught sight of his reflection in the mirror he could see how much he was perspiring.

Downstairs, he looked in on his father where he was lying with his eyes closed and his hand fisted outside the blankets. The old man did not wake and Morgan J was glad of it. Studying him though, he considered again what Mama Sox had told him. Who was Grandma Q? What did the old man want with her and how had he communicated it to Pious? He did not know the answers, but it was dawn already and there was no sign of Willow's mother so Chase and Peyton must have done their job. He no longer needed Noble. He did not need the codicil to his father's will; all he had to do was find Willow and to do that he had cross to Half-Mile Island.

———

Just before it got light Noble spotted the prowl car coming their way and it was moving very quickly. He knew immediately it was a sheriff's car because the red light above the windshield was reflected in the play from their headlights. He looked sideways at Grandma Q and she looked at him as he eased back on the throttle.

'If that's your brother you don't want to be dealing with him right now,' she said, 'so keep on going, Noble. Don't be slowing down any.'

They drove on and Noble shifted his weight where his trousers were sticking to the seat beneath him. His mouth was dry and he hunched up with his chin to his chest to try and avoid Chase recognising him. As they closed on the prowl car however, he could see there was only the driver up front and it was not Chase and it was not Peyton Skipwith either. The car was moving very quickly and it whizzed by without the driver giving them a sideways glance. Noble looked across and to his surprise, saw it was a woman at the wheel and not a sheriff's deputy.

'Did you see that, Mrs Q?' he asked her.

'Yes I did.'

'That was a woman driving.'

The old woman smiled now. 'That was Cassie Flood, Noble. Ain't quite sure what she's doing driving a sheriff's car, but like I said to you back at the house sometimes things have their own way of panning out and there ain't a damn thing we can do about it.'

———

John Q shot a wild pig. They needed to eat something for breakfast so he took the rifle and went to see what he could find. As he got to the top of the hill he found the hog snuffling through the long grass about half a mile from the settlement. Lying flat he levered a round into the chamber and shutting off his breath for a moment he sighted and when he was set he squeezed. The shot rang out, the gun kicked and the hog went down without so much as a squeal.

———

Morgan J heard that shot from where he was untying the boat at the Barra landing. Distant, it sounded faint like a single clap of thunder. He thought he knew where it came from and he knew then it had been smoke he'd seen just now and not a tendril of mist at all.

With a thin smile on his face he backed the boat away from the wooden jetty. Spinning the prow around, he pointed it downriver towards The Dividing aware that somehow that girl had gotten wind of what was going on and headed for her only place of sanctuary. That gunshot told him she was not alone and he figured she had Pious with her. From what Mama Sox liked to tell him her son knew that crossing as well as anyone and it was Pious whom his father had managed to speak to. How he had got hold of a gun he did not know or what he might be shooting at, but it was something to eat most probably. The whole thing reminded him of how it had been after Laurel was killed with Cassie making for the island every time she ran away from the Baptist cottages where she was supposed to be staying. Half-Mile Island was where his old man had found her when he decided to bring her into the family, but it was also where the

McHenry House had burned and where the McElroy's had been masters and Morgan J figured he knew it better than anyone.

———

Shouldering the hog, John Q carried it down to the village where he spotted Pious checking the boat for storm damage. John Q called to him. 'Hey, bud: set about that stove fire will you; got us some bacon here I need to skin out for breakfast.'

Willow appeared from the doorway of the hut. Dressed now, she looked at John Q and he looked at her and both were a little red in the cheekbone. 'Figure you were awake pretty early,' she told him.

'Guess I was,' John Q dropped the carcass of the hog onto a flattened tree stump he would use as a skinning board. 'Hungry Willow, are you?' he asked her.

'Famished.'

'Yeah, me too: listen, I need that fire built back so we can use the stove for cooking. Called down to Pious just now but maybe you could fix her and see if there ain't some old skillet somewheres we can use to broil bacon.'

'Sure,' she said. 'I'll get some more wood and see what I can find in the other cabins.'

He watched her go off to gather wood from the huts and then he set about skinning the wild pig with his clasp knife. He was about done when Pious came up the beach, his features grim and sallow.

'Forget about breakfast, John Q,' he said. 'We-all got us some company.'

Leaving the hog lying on the tree stump, John Q followed him down through the trees. Halfway across the channel he spied a motorboat heading their way and it was spilling a sizeable bow wave. One man at the wheel, for the first time John Q cast his gaze across Morgan Barra Junior. With a shake of his head he kicked at the dirt under his feet as if he wanted to kick himself. He looked back up the terrace to where he could see smoke drifting above the trees then he looked at the hog on the stump and the Winchester set against a tree. 'Damnit, John Q,' he muttered, 'if you ain't dumber than a donkey.'

Pious was staring across the water. 'Reckon he must've seen our smoke, huh; heard that shot; guess we all should've been more careful.'

John Q felt his cheeks redden and leaning to one side he spat. 'It ain't we, Pious. It's me.' He tugged at his lip with his teeth. 'I tell you, bud, if my godfather could see how I been acting just lately I figure he'd about disown me.'

He had to think now; he had to figure out what to do and he had to do it quickly. It was all very well telling his grandmother he was bringing the gun with him but there was Morgan Junior and in no time he would be on the beach and right now he had no clue what to do. Working his jaw he considered the lagoon and the shoreline, the settlement.

'All right then,' he said finally. 'We have to go get Willow and get out of here. He means to do her harm, Pious and you and me we got to protect her.'

———

Noble parked the car in the middle of Rutherford. They had only just got there on account of the road being blocked and the county clearing trees and power lines and it had taken longer than either of them had thought.

'Mrs Q.' he said, looking across the seat at her. 'When I left out of here last time it was from the county workhouse and I didn't plan on coming back anytime soon. Guess we're here now though, and you still ain't told me what we're doing.'

'No I haven't,' she agreed. 'I will, Noble I promise but only when I've got what I came for. I'll tell you all about it on the drive back to Spanish Fork.'

'We're going right back again then, are we?' He made a face: 'Figured if we had to come all this way we might at least hang around long enough to eat us a little breakfast.'

The old woman shook her head. 'Don't got time for breakfast. What say I cook you up something around lunchtime instead?' She turned her attention to the clock across the street on the wall of the library. 'Now,' she said, 'how long d'you figure before there'll be anybody over at the courthouse?'

———

Cassie drove the sheriff's prowl car the length of the driveway and pulling up outside the garage she all but fell out the door. Before she got to the house however, Mama Sox was in the yard with Eunice.

'Mrs Flood,' Mama stared at the automobile. She stared at Cassie's bedraggled appearance, her torn clothes and tangled hair, the mud across her hands and face. 'You look like somebody drug you through a ditch, ma'am. What happened to you and what-all you doing in a po-lice car?'

Cassie did not answer. 'Mama,' she said, 'where's Willow?'

The housekeeper's eyes were wide now, a little fear showing at the corners. 'Ma'am,' she said, 'fact is I ain't seen Miss Willow since yesterday.'

Cassie stood there for a moment staring at the open garage doors where the Cadillac was parked and the paintwork still spotted with rain-drops. She was conscious of panic building.

'Where's Morgan Junior?'

Mama shook her head. 'I ain't seen him either; not since I come across to the big house.'

'Where you been Mrs Flood?' Eunice asked her. 'Why you got a po-lice car and how come you is all so dirty?'

'Eunice,' Cassie bent to her. 'Have you seen Miss Willow?'

'No, ma'am,' Eunice shook her head. 'My brother said how we had to look out for her, but that was when it was storming.'

Cassie went into the house and hurriedly climbed the stairs. 'Willow?' she called. 'Willow?'

There was no answer.

'Morgan J?' she called. 'Are you up here?'

Still there was no answer.

She burst into her daughter's room but it was empty. The bed had not been slept in, the bathroom door was open but Willow wasn't there. The door to the balcony was ajar and the calico drape billowing. Stepping outside Cassie gazed the length of the garden. No sign, no hint of her daughter anywhere.

Striding across the landing she threw open Morgan Junior's door. That room too was empty though the bedclothes were rumpled up and the nightstand drawer pulled open. On the bed was a velvet bag and next to it a wooden box with Sam Colt's name printed on it. As her gaze fastened on it the blood seemed to rush at her temples.

Downstairs, she went into the study where her grandpa was awake and Cassie drew back the curtains. He lay in bed with his eyes fixed on her and saliva staining his lip. Gently Cassie took a piece of tissue to it. 'Grandpa,' she said, 'have you seen Willow?'

His eyes seemed to widen a fraction.

'Was she in here? Did Willow come and see you?'

He blinked now, very definitely.

'Is that a yes?'

Again he blinked. He opened his mouth and sucked air and she bent her head to see if he could whisper but no sound lifted.

'Grandpa,' she said. 'Morgan J just tried to kill me. He had Chase Landry grab me on the Rutherford Road, him and Peyton Skipwith. They dragged me into the forest and were going to murder me.' She laid a palm on his cheek. 'My mother,' she stammered, 'that night in the car it was Morgan J driving and she hadn't been drinking at all.' She stared at him with tears in her eyes. 'Did you know that? Is that why you adopted me? Is that why you changed your will so I'd inherit this place not Morgan Junior? They told me you changed your will. Chase and Peyton; they had me in the back of their prowl car and told me what you'd said to Morgan J. It's why they were trying to kill me.'

The old man could not answer. All he could do was look at her and she could see by the expression in his eyes that the frustration was almost killing him. She thought about what the doctor had said about a second stroke and the drugs she had fetched and how she did not have what she needed to administer them.

'It's all right,' she said. 'Don't take on. Right now it doesn't matter. You had your reasons, of course you did.' At the door she called Mama Sox. 'Mama, have Eunice run out to the car. The medicine is in the front. Have her bring it to me then call the doctor right away. Tell him we have the blood thinning drugs but we need him to come out here and give them to my grandpa. When you're done I want you to call Sheriff Carter in Rutherford and tell him he has to get over here.'

Mama sent Eunice out to fetch the drugs and Cassie turned back to her grandpa. 'I have to go now,' she said. 'I have to find Willow. Mama will take care of you and the doctor will be here very soon. I got the medicine you need, Grandpa; everything is going to be all right.'

He seemed to be trying to lift his hand, a curled knot of fingers where it lay outside the blankets.

Taking his hand Cassie held it. He looked up at her and he was desperately trying to speak. The frustration of not being able to brought tears to his eyes once more and gently Cassie soothed him. 'It's all right,' she said. 'Don't worry. It will all be all right. I'm going to find Willow. You just wait for the doctor.'

————

John Q followed Pious and Willow as they climbed the track where the ancient wagon ruts had just about been washed away. They made their way up the hill and as he glanced back he saw the motor boat cut between the Shark's Teeth into the lagoon. 'Pretty damn sure of himself ain't he.'

Pausing on the trail Pious looked where he did. 'Guess this is his island, John Q. There ain't nobody knows it like he does and I figure he thinks it'll be easy fetching out Miss Willow.' His brow furrowed them. 'I reckon he must've heard that shot though, and he don't know who's over here but he does know how they got a gun. That ought to make him a mite wary.'

'Yeah it should,' John Q was suddenly thoughtful. 'Pious,' he said. 'I got an idea. Why don't you go on ahead while I double back and see if I can't come up behind him?'

Pious looked doubtful. 'You sure you want to do that? You ain't your Uncle Frank just yet and you told me how Noble knew you were tailing him. What if he figures you're back there?'

'Pious, Morgan J ain't Noble Landry. Noble spent more time in the workhouse than any other kind of house I figure, and I'll be a sight more careful.' John Q gestured with the rifle. 'Go on,' he said. 'You two go ahead. Willow,' he called. 'Take Pious somewhere you can hide out now, someplace he ain't going to find you.'

Willow too looked doubtful. 'All right,' she said. 'But don't you think we ought to stick together?'

He shook his head. 'There's one of him and three of us only he don't know that does he. We need to let him think it's only you over here or you and Pious maybe. Pious ain't been home all night and it might be he knows that. A man like him, thinking the way he does, he's going to figure he's got things covered pretty good.' He spoke to Pious now. 'I know what I'm doing here, bud. You-all take off. I'll work my way around and come up again in back of him.'

Before they could argue he was gone, heading down the trail back the way they had come. When he got to the lip of the hill above the settlement he left the path and headed across country. The path bothered him as much as the gunshot and the trailing wood smoke. With all the rain having fallen, the dirt that had been hard baked was mush now and it carried their footprints. A couple of years back his Uncle Frank had started to teach him about prints and how they could tell a good tracker all kinds of things a lesser man would not be able to work out. Not just about where his prey was headed, but what kind of mood they were in, how bold they might be or how cautious. It was pretty clear from the dirt that there were three sets of tracks running that trail until halfway along the hilltop. There the three sets became only two and anybody with half a mind would be able to see that. He should've thought about it ahead of time and had Willow keep them off the footway.

It could not be helped now though, and he doubted Morgan J was an expert tracker anyway. Keeping well away from the trail, he went around the top of the hill and came at the slave village from the sandstone cliff. From there he could see the huts and he could see the lagoon, he could see the boat again only it was heading out to sea. That puzzled him and he stood there shading his eyes and saw that trailing behind was the skiff he and Pious had brought over. He watched as Morgan J made the passage between The Shark's teeth and then he was back in open water where he cracked the throttle and coasted the wave tops as far as Bull Shark Bay.

John Q watched him take a set of binoculars and make a sweep of the horizon. He watched him scanning every inch of that bay and every inch of the coastline also. He was looking for other boats, for anybody fishing from the shore. As far as John Q could see there was nobody out there and a few minutes later he watched as Morgan J brought the skiff alongside his boat, climbed in and bent to pull the bung out. Back in the bigger boat he opened up and rode hard again for the island.

The skiff was sinking; Morgan J had scuppered her and already she was low in the water. In a few minutes she would be gone altogether and when he got home Morgan J planned to tell everybody how Willow had drowned trying to cross The Dividing. Watching him, John Q was determined he would never tell that story. But unless they were able to take his boat somehow they were trapped on the island and the seriousness of the situation really struck him. This was no game they were playing, this was real-life and the rifle he was carrying confirmed it.

The motorboat came powering across the bay once more and Morgan J carried that passage as if the rocks beneath the surface did not exist. Moments later he was tying up a second time and John Q was aware of the way his heart was thumping.

Morgan J came striding up the jetty. On the beach he stood for a moment looking up and down and back the way he had come. Hidden in the trees John Q thought about that old coyote his Uncle Frank liked to refer to. He looked on with the rifle gripped in both hands and a round levered into the chamber. His heartbeat seemed so loud it was ringing out like a dinner gong. It was about all he could hear right now and he had to keep wiping his hands on his jeans where the palms were sweating.

Morgan J wore a gabardine jacket with the zipper undone and the collar turned under his chin. He wore sunglasses that glinted every now and again when the sun caught the lenses. He was cautious, looking up and down the beach, peering into the trees that had overtaken most of the slave huts. John Q could see where smoke still lifted from Mama Sox's.

Morgan J was studying that smoke and as he stood there he took a pistol from his waistband and checked the magazine. With his mouth suddenly drained of saliva John Q tightened his grip around the stock of the rifle and thought about how long it would be before his grandma called the sheriff. How long before she figured he and Pious were missing?

———

TWENTY-FOUR

Grandma Q came out of the courthouse in Rutherford and walked down the steps to where Noble was waiting. He got out of the car and made his way around the front to help her into the passenger seat. Then he cranked the engine. When he got behind the wheel again she had the codicil to Morgan Barra's will in her hand along with another document.

'What you got there, Mrs Q?' Noble asked her.

'Something Morgan Barra wanted to give me back at the house but couldn't on account of he wasn't able to tell me where he'd hidden it. I told him it didn't matter. I told him all we had to do was drive up here and I'd have someone in the courthouse get on the telephone to Atlanta.' She looked at him then with a smile. 'Now I got this copy typed up we need to go over to the sheriff's department real quick because there ain't but one reason Cassie Flood would be driving a prowl car.'

Noble was silent. He stared at the gap where the windshield did not quite meet the roof, it was where water had been coming in most of the journey and he was wondering if they ought just to take the top down altogether now that it had stopped raining.

'Sheriff's department,' he uttered slowly. 'Mrs Q, you ain't saying as how you want me to come in there with you?'

She shifted round in the seat. 'Noble,' she said. 'Wasn't it just a few hours ago you got done telling me how it was you'd been taking the blame for what your older brother been doing? Every time there was any kind of jam it was you he made scapegoat, particularly since you got out of the army.'

He nodded.

'So was that true or was it just a bunch of bullshit?'

He gawped at her use of language. 'It was true,' he said. 'I done told it how it was exactly.'

'So think on this then,' she suggested. 'Your brother's had his time: him and Peyton both. I figure those two boys been running our part of the county ever since Cassie Flood's mother drowned in The Pit.' She gestured through the windshield. 'I figure it's time the folk in Spanish Fork got to hear the truth about what-all they been doing and I figure it's time they heard the truth about you, Noble Landry. Fact is it ain't Chase been working the chain gang these past six months and it ain't Peyton Skipwith been living in a broken down Pullman.' She looked hard at him then. 'Now, we're going to swing by the sheriff's office. When we get there whether you come in or not, whether you got anything to say, I'll leave that up to you.'

———

On the island John Q crept between the trees. He could smell cigar smoke, had caught a sudden whiff of it and hunkered down behind a rock above Mama Sox's cabin. He heard somebody cough and there he was barely a few paces from where John Q was hiding. Morgan Junior, he held a thin black cigar in one hand and as John Q watched he pressed the pistol back into his waistband.

John Q barely took a breath. Morgan J stood there and sucked on that cigar and let smoke drift. Then he disappeared inside the hut and a few minutes later he came out again and scanned the lagoon once more and the bay.

He set out walking the length of that terrace back the way he had come. John Q remained where he was and now he was only able to spot Morgan J intermittently. He saw him make the trail though, watched him start up it and saw him again as he drew level with the terrace where John Q was hiding. His chin was high and he was looking up the hill and not at the ground at his feet. If he looked at the ground he would pick up their tracks and John Q cursed himself for not thinking about that before they started.

———

Cassie crossed the lawn to the wooden steps at the bottom of the garden. Taking them carefully she started down but long before she got to the river she could see that two of the three boats were missing.

She could barely take it in and for a moment she just stood there trembling. The third boat was old and had been berthed a long time without ever being started and she knew that any gasoline in the tank would long since have evaporated. Biting her lip, she thought about her daughter and how bad the weather had been last night and how it must have been in the bay. In her mind's eye she could see her capsizing. She could see her in the water floundering, desperate and she pushed the images away. Turning again she went back up the steps and crossed the lawn to the garage where Albert was washing the Cadillac.

'Albert,' she said. 'Two boats are gone from the mooring.'

He looked up at her and his gaze was wary. 'Mrs Flood,' he said, 'last night all everybody was looking for Miss Willow. If that small boat ain't there then I figure she took it. If the big one ain't there,' he gestured, 'then I guess that has to be Mr Morgan.'

Eyes closed for a second Cassie just stood there. 'The other one,' she said, 'the old one; can you get her started?'

'Figure I can though she surely ain't got no gas in her. I'll have to go into town to get some.'

She nodded. 'Go on then. Take the car and fetch some gas. But get back here as fast as you can.'

———

Together Pious and Willow made it to the grounds of the McElroy Mansion. They scoured the area for a hiding place and Pious spotted a beaten up old corn crib built in the lee of a hut about halfway along the overgrown avenue. Willow suggested they go into the house itself but Pious disagreed. He told her Morgan J would probably figure they would do that and search it before he looked anywhere else. He said the corn crib was better because it was so tangled up with weed you could hardly make it out all. It was cramped inside though, and he checked for coral snakes before they climbed in. There were gaps in the sides where patches of the animal dung daub had long since fallen away and they could see a good way back up the trail.

Pious still had the oilskin bag and the flare gun. 'I guess your momma must've showed you how to use this,' he stated, looking the gun over, 'in case you-all got stuck over here or something.'

Taking it from him now, Willow considered where the barrel was a lot stubbier than the handle. 'Yes she did,' she said. 'She taught me how to shoot it.' She indicated the foremost of two flared hammers and told him it was called the mount latch. Popping it back she did the same with the lower hammer and the barrel hinged open. 'Have you got a flare in that bag?' she asked him.

Rooting around for a moment Pious handed her a cartridge, like those for a shotgun only it was much fatter. Willow slotted it into the barrel and snapped it closed then held the gun in both hands.

'Now all you have to do is pull the trigger.' She passed it back to him and instead of stowing it in the bag Pious stuffed it in the waistband of his pants and covered the handle with the hem of his shirt.

For a while after that they were silent. On her haunches Willow peered through the gaps in the wall. 'Pious,' she said. 'I figure it was corn cribs like this that brought those bears over I was telling you about. It stinks in here and I reckon a bear could pick up on that smell at least ten miles upriver, don't you?'

She was quiet again as Pious lifted a finger to his lips. Then he pointed through a hole in the wall and Willow spotted Morgan Junior about fifty yards back up the trail. He stood there surveying the grounds to his ancestor's mansion before cupping a hand to his mouth and calling out.

'Willow? Are you here? Come on out for goodness sake. Your mother's worried to death about you.'

When he mentioned her mother Willow stiffened. Eyes balled she watched him as he came down the trail and halted right alongside the corn crib. Not six feet from where they were hiding his gaze flitted from the broken down huts to the facade of the mansion and the sign he had hung years before.

'Condemned you shall be,' he muttered, 'though I guess momma would like it if I fixed up the house. Who knows maybe I will, could make a hotel out of the place or something.' He was talking to himself and then he called again. 'Willow, your mother's home from Rutherford and she's very worried about you. She got caught out in the storm but she made it back with my dad's medicine. She's on her way over here herself. Come on now; I don't know why you ran off like you did but I told her I'd bring you down to the jetty.'

In the crib they remained as still as they could, watching Morgan J as he stood with his hands on his hips and his gaze fixed on the house. Then his gaze shifted and he glanced briefly at the huts and the undergrowth before he set off down the path once more. They watched him, lost him then picked him out again through the gaps in the other wall.

'If he goes in the house we get out of here,' Pious said. 'Miss Willow, if he goes inside we head on back to the beach.'

For the next few minutes they kept their faces pressed to the wall but could no longer see Morgan J. Willow glanced at Pious. 'Did he go in the house already?'

'I don't know, I didn't see.'

'Let's give it another minute then go.'

They hunched there. They waited. Then finally Pious touched Willow on the shoulder and she looked up as he lifted the doors. The crib was rectangular with the back wall taller than the front and the doors fitted on the slant. Easing himself out Pious looked up and down the path but there was no sign of Morgan J. Glancing back, he nodded to Willow and she climbed out now and they stood in the lee of the hut.

'Did you see where he went?' Willow whispered.

'Nope; there ain't no sign.'

She looked back the way they had come then she gestured to the next hut about twenty yards up the path.

'Let's make our way back,' she said. 'Flit from one to the next. If we spot him we can duck inside.'

'Good idea,' Pious led the way, keeping off the path and moving through the scrub where the grass was knee high. He was almost at the door of the second hut when Morgan J appeared on the other side.

He had doubled back, must've heard them climb out of the crib and come around again. He hadn't seen Willow but he was staring at Pious now. 'Boy,' he said, 'just what do you think you're doing?'

Pious was rooted. Willow was rooted. Moving quickly Morgan J strode up to Pious then he spotted Willow and his eyes narrowed into points of light.

'Willow,' he said, 'didn't you hear me calling? I've been looking for you. Everybody has. Your mother is on her way over.' He smiled then and he gestured. 'Didn't you hear me? You must've heard me. Look, I have no idea what you thought you were doing taking a boat out in a storm but I figured it'd be here you'd come and that's what I told your mother.'

Willow did not say anything. She just looked at him with her lips pressed tightly together.

Hands on his hips he was smiling. 'I've come to fetch you back. I've come to take you home now.'

Still Willow held his eye then she looked at Pious. 'Is my mother all right?'

'Of course she is; she's fine. Why wouldn't she be? She got back from Rutherford and she's been waiting for you ever since. She's worried though,' he said, 'really worried. What were you thinking about coming over here in the kind of weather we had going last night?' Brow furrowed, he gesticulated towards the water. 'I saw a skiff smashed on the rocks. I thought it was you but then I saw your boat moored at the dock so it couldn't have been.' He looked at Pious. 'Were you in that other boat?'

Pious shook his head.

'Must be an old wreck then, something the storm dragged up.'

Pious glanced briefly at Willow.

'I don't know what you think you were doing worrying everybody like that,' Morgan J went on. 'What possessed you to come over here when that kind of storm was raging?'

She looked at him. She lifted her shoulders. She didn't say anything.

'Well anyway, it doesn't matter,' still he was smiling. 'You're safe and that's all that counts. But your mother is beside herself with worry. Come on,' he said, 'let's get you back to the lagoon. I'm sure she'll be on her way over.'

He led the way up the hill and, not sure what else to do, Pious and Willow followed. They walked the path through the woods to the escarpment where the bay lay bathed in sunlight and the waters of the lagoon glimmered blue.

There Willow paused. For a long moment she stared. The jetty, the point where John Q and Pious had tied up her boat, there was something wrong with that picture but it took a moment to register what it was. And then all at once she knew. The skiff was gone. There was only the big boat moored there now.

Heart pounding suddenly she twisted round to where Morgan J had walked behind them. His eyes were cold and in his hand he held a pistol.

'It's gone,' he said, 'your boat, Willow; that's what you're looking for, right? It sank up in Bull Shark Bay.'

'What?' she stammered. 'What're you talking about?'

'You and the boy here,' he gestured, lifted his shoulders, 'for some fool reason you tried to cross The Dividing in the worst storm we've had in years and you were shunted off course. You lost power maybe, engine cut out and you drifted. You ended up in Bull Shark Bay and with the waves the way they were that's when the boat began to take on water.'

Willow was trembling. Next to her Pious was trembling. Morgan J indicated the trail down to the settlement with the gun.

'Go on,' he said, 'get moving the pair of you. Go on.'

They didn't move. They couldn't move. They just stood where they were and his gaze dulled still further. 'Move,' he repeated. 'Go on, down the hill with you.'

They had no choice but to do what he said and with Pious taking the lead, they started down the trail.

'When I get home I'll have to tell the sheriff how I searched and searched but I just couldn't find you,' Morgan J stated sadly. 'That little boat was gone and no matter where I looked there was nothing. A tragedy, awful; drowned I guess or eaten by the bull sharks maybe.'

———

TWENTY-FIVE

John Q waited until they had made it beyond the line of trees. He waited till they were on the beach almost heading for the little wooden jetty. He still wasn't sure how he was going to handle this but Morgan J had a gun on his friends and he had to do something. Desperately he tried to think what his godfather would advise then he stepped out from behind the tree where he had been hiding. Not sure of his voice he called out regardless.

'Mr Barra,' he said. 'I guess you better stop right there.'

Morgan J paused mid-step. He had Willow just in front of him and in a flash he had grabbed her by the shoulder. The movement was so sudden there was nothing John Q could do. Spinning round to face him, Morgan J had an arm across Willow's throat and the pistol pressed to her temple.

'The one with the gun,' he said. 'You little fool; I heard that shot all the way from the river landing.'

Swallowing hard now John Q stared at him.

'What with that and the wood smoke, the three sets of tracks on the trail: for God's sake, boy; put that gun down before you shoot your foot off or something.'

John Q stood where he was.

'Put it down,' Morgan J told him. 'There is nothing you can do here now.'

John Q glanced at Willow. 'Mr Barra,' he said. 'I ain't going to let you hurt her.'

'No? So what're you going to do then, shoot me? I don't think so; not without hitting her and you don't want to do that, do you.' His expression was derisory suddenly. 'Put the rifle down now before I lose my temper.'

For a moment longer John Q held his ground. His heart was work-ing in his chest and his mouth was dry and he knew that with a pistol to Willow's head like that he really didn't have a choice. From the corner of his eye however, he could see Pious had stepped back a few paces and was working a palm from his thigh to his waistband. Morgan J was so busy watching him he did not take any notice of Pious.

'All right, Mr Barra,' John Q said finally. 'I'm going to put the rifle down like you said.' Carefully, slowly, keeping his gaze fixed on Morgan J's face, he laid the gun on the sand.

'Sensible boy,' Morgan J said, 'now I want all three of you to get in my boat. Pious, you can take the wheel while I......' He looked round now and saw Pious with the flare gun pointed at him.

'Oh, for heaven's sake.' Morgan J gawped at him. 'You really are begin-ning to get on my nerves now.'

'Let Miss Willow go,' Pious said. 'I figure you going to drown us any-way. Take us out to the bay and drop us over the side for the bull sharks to chew on some. That's how you told it up on the hill just now.' He looked Morgan J in the eye. 'Well, I been thinking about that and there ain't no way I'm going to get ate by a shark so you might as well be shooting us instead.'

'Don't be a fool,' Morgan J told him, 'put that gun down before some-thing happens here you'll regret.'

'What he'll regret maybe is how we get in the boat and you run us out there like he said,' John Q spoke now. 'He's got a point, sir. I mean what's it matter whether you shoot us or drown us, either way we'll end up dead.' He looked down once more at his rifle.

'Now you listen.' Morgan J's gaze flitted across him before settling on Pious again. 'Boy,' he said, 'put that flare gun down right now. Do you hear me?'

Pious did not put it down. He held his ground and Morgan J stood there with his face beginning to boil red. He opened his mouth. He closed it again then shifting the gun from where he had it pointed at Willow he aimed it at Pious instead.

Willow took her chance, kicking back on his shin she twisted free of his grip and half fell stumbling away from him. With a cry of rage, Morgan J swung the pistol towards her then back at Pious as if he couldn't make up his mind who to shoot. In that moment John Q dived for the rifle. Morgan J fired at him instead and the bullet kicked up a puff of wet sand. Eyes on stalks, Pious fired the flare gun. Deliberately aiming high, the round whooshed into the air and exploded overhead.

Instinctively Morgan J ducked.

When he came up again John Q had the Winchester levelled at him but before he knew it Morgan J had fired again. John Q could not believe it, the bullet whizzing so close he felt the wind rush on the skin of his arm. Face the color of beetroot, Morgan J went to fire a third time but the gun jammed and John Q worked the action on his rifle.

'Mr Barra,' he said. 'Bring that piece up again and I swear I will cut you down so help me God.'

———

TWENTY-SIX

Albert was down at the jetty with the can of gasoline trying to get the old launch started when he saw Morgan J's boat racing upriver. He could see Pious at the wheel and Willow sitting there as well as another kid. As far as Albert could see that kid had a rifle and it looked for-all-the-world like he was holding it on Morgan Junior. Scratching his head, Albert started up the steps to the house.

From the patio, Cassie heard vehicles rumble up the driveway. Crossing the lawn she spotted a Model T Ford with a pair black and white painted sheriff's vehicles following behind it.

The Ford pulled up and Cassie realised it was Noble Landry driving with Grandma Q in the passenger seat and that did not make any sense. Behind them the first of the prowl cars came to a stop and Sheriff Carter got out. In the back Cassie could see Chase Landry with his hands cuffed behind him. Two more deputies climbed from the second car and Cassie looked from them to where Grandma Q had got down from the Model T.

'What's going on?' she said. 'Mrs Q, I don't understand.'

'Just drove over from Rutherford,' the old woman told her. 'Spotted your car where the road was out, I guess the county will tow her. Cassie, me and Noble saw you-all driving that prowl car.' She pointed to where Chase Landry's vehicle was parked. 'Thought it a little odd so I swung by Sheriff Carter's office and he said how Mama Sox called him already and he was on his way out.' She took Cassie's arm now. 'Down the road there we found old Chase looking like a cowboy done lost his horse.

Peyton too, though he couldn't stand up on account of how he'd busted a hip.'

———

John Q was on his feet as Pious guided the boat up to the Barra landing. They came alongside and rifle in hand, John Q jumped out to tie the rope. Momentarily he had his back to Morgan J and Morgan J made a lunge for Willow. She was half out of the boat already and he sent her sprawling onto the dock. Fists clenched, Pious came at him but he grabbed the boy by the shoulders and marched him backwards so hard his calves slapped the gunwales, his knees buckled and he went over the side with a splash. The engine was still running and grabbing the wheel, Morgan J spun the boat about.

Pious was floundering, just about keeping his head above the surface; he managed to swim clear before he got mashed by the boat. Willow was on the jetty and John Q helped her to her feet. He watched as Morgan J opened the throttle and took off upriver.

'Shoot him,' Pious yelled through a mouthful of muddy water. 'Shoot him, John Q. Shoot him for Christ's sake.'

'Pious, I ain't going to shoot him,' John Q called back. 'He don't got a gun and I ain't shooting nobody who don't got a gun. I reckon the sheriff can catch up to him. Right now we got to get Willow up to the house.'

Reaching down he grabbed Pious's hand and hauled him out of the river. Pious stood on the jetty like half-drowned rat with water pouring off his clothes where it formed a puddle at his feet. Together they watched the boat till it took the first of the bends and then only the foam from its wake was left.

'Sheriff will pick him up,' John Q reiterated. 'Sumbuck almost ran you down there, bud, you okay, are you?'

Pious nodded grimly. 'Little wet is all but it ain't as if I ain't been wet before now is it.'

'There you go,' John Q slapped him on the back. Then turning to Willow he took her hand. 'Come on,' he said. 'Let's go see what's happening up at the house.'

As they got to the top of the stairway they saw Willow's mother on the patio and she looked up, let out a cry and came running across the lawn. Willow burst into tears and fell into her arms and they just stood there holding each other.

Beyond the pool, John Q could see his grandmother along with the sheriff and a bunch of uniformed deputies.

'Johnny,' his grandma called, 'son, are you all right?'

'I'm just fine, Grandma,' he told her. He carried the Winchester in his hand still and, crossing the grass, he spoke to the sheriff.

'Sir,' he said. 'Morgan Junior just took off in a boat. He was going to kill Willow and Pious and he took a couple of shots at me. We were bringing him in but he knocked Pious in the water just now and took off in the boat.'

The sheriff looked at him with his brows knit deeply. 'All right, son,' he said. 'Which way did he go?'

'Upriver I reckon though I guess he could've doubled back.'

Together with his deputies the sheriff went back to their cars. Mama Sox took Pious off to get some dry clothes and at the behest of John Q's grandma, the rest of them gathered in Mr Barra's study. She told them she had things to say and that they should sit down and get comfortable because it might take a while. Willow and her mother perched on the little couch close to the bed where Mr Barra was propped up on his pillows. Leaning the rifle against the wall, John Q stood in the open doorway.

His gaze was fixed on Willow and he could still feel the warmth of her hand where he had held it as they climbed the steps from the jetty. She smiled at him briefly then she turned to his grandma who was studying a document she told them she had fetched from the courthouse in

Rutherford. Briefly now she looked at Mr Barra then she turned to Willow and her mother.

'There are things I have to say to you two,' she began, 'things Mr Barra wanted to tell you himself but he can't now on account of his stroke. Cassie,' she sighed, 'it was the day of your mother's memorial we spoke about it first. I was on the bridge with the folk from Half-Mile Island and Mr Barra came by to pay his respects like the gentleman he always was. I told him that there were things he ought to know and he told me to come up here to the house but he had to go to the hospital in Rutherford first.' She glanced at the old man again. 'When I got up here that evening he told me how he bumped into Peyton Skipwith in the parking lot and that was the same day his testimony was printed in the newspaper. Mr Barra told me what happened after he left Peyton and went up to see Morgan J.'

———

Having left the deputy standing by his car Mr Barra went up to the room where his son was recovering from broken ribs and a dislocated shoulder. A bone in his right leg was cracked and he was in a lot of pain. His room was on the second floor and when his father went in Morgan J was propped up in bed with his torso strapped and his arm was wrapped in a sling.

'What say, Dad? You got a cigarette there do you, I'm jonesing.'

Hands in his pockets, his father considered him. 'I spoke to Deputy Skipwith outside in the parking lot. He told me what happened the other night and it's about what I read this morning in the newspaper. But then I guess he'd make sure his stories matched and it would be exactly what you told him to say now, wouldn't it?'

Morgan J half-lifted an eyebrow. 'What're you talking about?'

'I'm talking about Peyton Skipwith and Chase Landry. I'm talking about how you've got those two good old boys in your pocket.'

'Sure I do,' Morgan J told him. 'On account of I'm a Barra and we own half the county and people like us always have the cops in our pocket. But that's not what this is about. I didn't tell either one of them boys to say anything.'

'Sure you did,' his father stated. 'You told them to say exactly what was printed in the newspaper.'

Morgan J looked at him now with his lip curled and his father stepped to the window. Hands in his pockets he stood with his back to the bed.

'What's on your mind old man?' Morgan J asked him. 'You and I never did see eye to eye but what's bugging you now particularly?'

His father spoke without turning. 'What's on my mind is a ten year old girl whose mother was drowned in The Pit. What's bugging me is how that little girl looked just now as she tossed flowers she'd picked, from the bridge.'

'You went to the funeral of a squatter?' His son sounded incredulous.

His father turned from the window and when he spoke he seemed to punch each word from between his teeth. 'I went to the memorial is what I did. That's all they can have on account of there's no recovering Laurel Brown's body. That squatter had a name; Morgan J. You ought to know, you've been living with her all summer, hiding over there while I squared away your debts in Atlantic City.'

'You paid off the tables?' Morgan worked himself up on one elbow. 'Well I'll be. Guess I ought to thank you, Daddy.' His eyes darkened again. 'But it ain't really you paying them off now, is it? I'm good for that money, just don't have it in cash right now on account of you digging your heels in when it comes to developing the island.' A little bitterly he shook his head. 'My mother's money; all her holdings in your name and I got no access to any of it.

'Doesn't seem fair really, does it? I mean who were you before she married you? She was the one with the money. She was the McElroy and it was the McElroys that owned all the property.' Sitting higher in the bed still, he jabbed an index finger. 'It's a fact you only married into the family whereas I got that blood flowing right here in me.'

'Yes you do,' his father told him. 'And if your mother knew how you'd been these last few years she would be regretting she ever gave birth to you.' He studied him then very coldly. 'You were driving that car, Morgan J. There's no way that girl was behind the wheel because she'd never have been able to get her primed and she could never have cranked that handle. I know what goes on at Willy Koontz' place and I know you were drunk and it was you *driving that vehicle and it was you that wrecked on Bluff Bridge. Right now you've got those deputies covering for you with the coroner and the newspapers but you ran off the road with that poor woman sitting next to you only she wasn't as lucky as you. She's still down there in that whirlpool right now and her bones at least, always will be.'*

For a long time after that he was silent, his eyes wrinkled up at the corners. 'I heard it said somewhere that the sins of the father are visited upon the son. Well with you and me it's the other way round.' Now he bent to the bed. 'I want you to listen to me and I want you to listen well. You're a liar, Morgan J. It's habitual. You'll say anything to anybody to get what you want and if your mother were alive I think she'd probably disown you.' He paused for a moment before he went on. 'Let me promise you something right here. Let me promise you I'm going to do whatever I can for that child you orphaned if only to remind me of what you did.'

————

In the study Grandma Q turned to the old man where he lay against his pillows now. 'That's how you told it to me, right, sir, that's about what you said?'

The old man blinked once, and, turning from him, Grandma Q considered Cassie for a moment before she spoke to Willow. 'Honey,' she said, 'you thought your great-grandpa was trying to tell you something and the fact of it all is he was. What he was trying to say was not the fact that he had changed his will so much though, as the reason why. What he wanted you to know is that it's been a long time since he trusted Morgan Junior and it was time you and your mother knew the truth. His only problem was he couldn't tell you now because he'd had a stroke.' She looked beyond them then through the open patio doors to the apartment above the garage. 'Somehow, by the grace of God maybe, he managed to get hold of me through young Pious instead.' She sighed then. She made an open-handed gesture. 'I'd known all along of course because after what he told me about that visit to the hospital, I told him how it really was.'

Finally she passed the document she was holding to Cassie. 'Sweetheart,' she said. 'That's what your grandpa was trying to tell Willow about. He wanted her to find it and give it to you only he wasn't able to make her understand. That's a copy right there. I had them make it for me at the courthouse over in Rutherford this morning because the original is in this house somewhere only Mr Barra couldn't tell me where it is any-more than he could tell Willow.' She smiled then widely. 'It didn't matter. You see when I got here I already knew what it was he wanted to see me about because we'd talked about it long ago.'

Cassie was staring at the sheet of paper, head down; her hands were shaking and her lips seemed very thin. Sitting next to her Willow had her brow wrinkled as she too looked at the page.

'Birth certificate,' she said.

'That's right it's a birth certificate; one I signed off on thirty some years ago.' Grandma Q was nodding now where she stood. 'Willow, Mr Barra didn't adopt your mother, through Morgan Junior she was already his.'

For a long time after that nobody spoke. Where he was standing at the open door John Q wasn't sure if he had figured it right, but his grand-mother smiled at him and he knew that he had.

'Cassie,' Grandma Q said turning to her once again. 'When he came to fetch you from the orphanage in Rutherford that last time your grandpa was bringing you home. Only he never got around to telling you the truth and he never got around to telling his son. I guess he always meant to. I guess the day he told Morgan J he wasn't getting the money he intended to tell him who you really were and why the estate was by-passing him. If he'd been able to do that and if Morgan J had only thought it through, he might've understood. Only it never happened. He stormed off before his father had a chance to explain and a couple of hours later your grandpa was struck down by the stroke.

'He swore me to secrecy,' she said; 'not because of what people round here might think but because he knew his son. He knew that the last thing you needed right then was the kind of father Morgan J would've been so he was your guardian instead.'

Still smarting from what it actually meant John Q was staring at Willow and she was staring wide-eyed at him. He glanced at Mr Barra then and could see how the old man was concentrating on every word his grandmother said.

'I'm sure you were meant to know long before now,' she went on, 'but he held off telling you because I don't think he wanted to burden you with it all.'

Willow's mother looked up at her and her hands were shaking where she gripped the paper still.

'He didn't know how you would react if you found out that your father had been responsible for your mother's death. So time went on and you got married and he still hadn't gotten around to it yet. Then your husband went off to war and, like my husband, he never came back.' Lifting her palms Grandma Q spread them a little helplessly before her. 'He just put it off and put it off on account of how there had been so much pain and death.'

A little wearily she sat down at the old man's desk. 'Anyway,' she finished, 'that's how it was. That day of the memorial your grandpa told me how he would call me if he ever needed me to tell you and I guess that's what he did. There was no other way. He couldn't make you understand but he knew I could get a copy of the birth certificate because I was the midwife and it was me who registered who the father was. I'm sorry you had to find out this way, Cassie, but at least now you know the truth.'

Leaving the three of them together in the study she led John Q out into the sunshine where Noble was sitting by the swimming pool, making a cigarette.

'Been driving me all over,' the old woman said. 'Noble, I mean. Talked to the sheriff over in Rutherford, told him what happened with his brother and Morgan J. Admitted how he'd broken into that attorney's office and stole the codicil like he did. Sheriff's going to take it all in mitigation, talk to the county attorney and see if they won't leave it at that. Folk underestimate Noble Landry, Johnny; he only did what he did on account of how he was desperate, I guess.' She paused then and looked towards him again. 'When all this is done with I might talk to Cassie about him and some kind of job.' She nodded towards the garage. 'Albert ain't getting any younger so unless it's Pious going to do all the work there might be something here for him.'

They crossed to where Noble had lit his cigarette and then Pious came down from the upstairs apartment wearing dry clothes. A few minutes later Mama Sox came out from the kitchen of the big house with a pitcher of iced lemonade.

John Q could still hardly take it all in. Pouring a glass of lemonade he stood for a moment looking the length of the yard only not seeing anything much.

Pious laid a hand on his shoulder. 'Penny for them, John Q,' he said.

'Cost you a whole lot more than that right now.' John Q looked back. 'You okay, bud? Dried off proper then, are you, huh?'

Pious nodded.

'What say, Noble?' John Q turned to him then. 'Grandma told me how you been driving her around and everything. I reckon Willow and her mom need some time together right now, so how about you-all take us back to the house?'

Walking to the car a yawn took him suddenly and he worked the heel of a hand across his face. 'Could sleep for a week already but now this rain quit falling I got me a house to paint.'

'I could give you a hand if you want,' Pious suggested. He looked at Grandma Q. 'If you want, ma'am, I could give John Q a hand with your house painting. Wouldn't want paying or nothing, just be a favor, I guess.'

'Well, that would sure help to get her done double quick.' The old woman smiled at him. 'It's kind of you, Pious, and if you're volunteering I think that's a fine idea. Get her done and I reckon you two boys got the rest of the summer to yourselves afterwards and there's an island you ain't started exploring yet.'

'You mean that, Grandma?' John Q said.

'Sure I mean it. Wouldn't say her if I didn't and you told me how you're going to go cowboy soon as you get back. You're only young once and now you quit school I figure this summer's the last you're going to have before you're grown up.'

At the car Noble set the throttle to prime then walked around the front and made a half turn with the crank.

John Q was sitting in the back with Pious and his grandmother turned to him now. 'So that sumbuck took a shot at you then?'

'Two actually, both of them missed and the pistol jammed after that.'

'You were lucky.'

'Yes ma'am, I guess.'

She squinted at him. 'Did your Uncle Frank ever tell you how many times he'd been shot at?'

'No ma'am, he don't talk about stuff like that.'

'Far as I recall last count it was seventeen, that's how many times he was hit anyways and on four occasions they left him for dead.'

Back in the driver's seat Noble engaged reverse. John Q could see how much he was enjoying driving as he pointed the Ford's nose west.

'So Morgan Junior is kin to a squatter,' Noble said. 'Never would've guessed anything like that.'

'Careful who you're calling squatter, Noble Landry,' Grandma Q told him. 'Last time I looked nobody'd invited you to take up residence down where you did.'

From the pocket of her dress she brought out her pipe. 'I figured something was going on right back when they got me over to the island for Cassie's birth. Pious, it was your mama doing the chatter; ten years old back then, she could talk almost as much as she does now.' She took a pinch of tobacco to her pipe. 'Told me how Morgan J had been around earlier in the year; how he'd been threatening them and how it was only Laurel could ever calm him down. Told me he'd been staying with her in her cabin and over there on the island folk didn't ask a whole lot of questions and who anybody was sleeping with was nobody's business but their own.' She tamped the bowl with her thumb. 'Wasn't like that on the mainland of course, but the island had its own ways. Slow up a little will you, Noble, I need to get this lit.'

They were on the highway now and Noble slowed the car and Grandma Q took a match to her pipe. 'Laurel confirmed how it was with the father and all after Cassie was born. She told me Morgan J was the one but she never wanted him to know on account of who he was and she was terrified they might take the baby away.'

'I guess he's going to find out,' John Q said from where he sat in the back, 'when the sheriff gets a-hold of him it's going to be quite a shock.'

'Yes it is,' his grandma blew smoke. 'That's why the old man wanted that paperwork so badly. It's how he managed to whisper my name. He knew I was the only person who knew about it and like I said, years back we had talked it all through.' Her eyes darkened fractionally then. 'Trouble is, even if he had known who Cassie and Willow were I don't think it would've stopped Morgan J.'

Eyes wide, Noble looked sideways at her now. 'You don't?'

'No, sir: I'm afraid I don't.'

They were silent the four of them after that. In the back John Q was thinking about what his mother had told him before he left San Saba County to come out.

'Grandma,' he said, 'before I left out to catch the bus my mom told me that who a person is, their personality and everything, is pretty much fixed by the time they're seven years old. She said that the rest of who they end up being is figured out by what happens to them and the people they meet on the way.'

'Did she say that?' His grandma took another match to her pipe.

'Yes ma'am, she did.

'And do you understand what it is she meant?'

'Well ma'am, I didn't at first, bugged me the whole way out.'

'And what about now?'

'Now I got a notion for sure.'

———

TWENTY-SEVEN

That same night Morgan J hovered in the shadows of Miller's Town station a few miles upriver from Spanish Fork. He was watching the porter preparing for the approaching train that would take him north and out of the state. He shifted uneasily; one foot to the other, looking up and down the platform he was keeping an eye out for cops. Earlier he had bought a cup of coffee in the drugstore across the street where he heard on the radio how the Light Horse County Sheriff had a warrant out on him and had issued an "all points".

In the distance he heard the train whistle and he could smell smoke. Then he saw the headlamp where the cow catcher was just about visible at the front. It was dark already and the lights were shining on the platform where the handful of people waiting, started getting up.

Still Morgan J hung back. Still he was looking for any sign of cops. There were none though, and he was thinking, plotting; aware that Willow's mother was still alive and how a couple of kids who weren't fifteen yet had somehow managed to take him out. He figured Spanish Fork had reporters crawling all over the place right now and he needed to get out of Georgia and find somewhere he could hole up.

The train came to a stop and the doors opened. Keeping his chin low, Morgan J followed a young woman and her son as they got aboard and when they paused at the door he pushed past. He walked up the corridor and found a seat among four that were empty and slumped down next to the glass.

He closed his eyes, exhaustion overtaking him and when he opened them again they were already underway.

Three young black men wearing slick looking business suits were gathered in the seats around him. Staring from one to the other he felt his heart miss a beat.

'Morgan J,' Shoofly was seated directly opposite, 'can't say it's a pleasant surprise. Not sure it even is a surprise but I'm glad to see you either way.'

Morgan J just stared at him.

'Po-lice made sure me and the boys caught this train out from Spanish Fork. Seems the way a black man is treated down here is even worse than it is back in Jersey. Don't you people know how we got the vote?' He sat forward then with his hands clasped. 'Wondered if I might run into you though; heard how you messed up and there was a warrant out.'

'You'll get your money, Shoofly.'

'No sir, I rather think I won't.'

'Of course you will,' Morgan J said. 'My father is still alive. I can talk to him; tell him what's gone down here, he's not going to just sit tight.'

'Oh but he is, Morgan J: that's the point.'

'What're you talking about? He's my old man. He's not got to let me die.'

'There ain't nothing he can do. He can't stop it and he ain't going to come up with any dough. You're mine now, you belong to me; he ain't going to bail you out.'

'Shoofly,' Morgan J was sweating, 'you don't know what you're talking about.'

'Sure I do. Maybe it's you that don't.'

'What do you mean?'

Shoofly smiled only his eyes were dark. 'I mean those two you tried to get rid of, the woman and her little girl. They're kin to him on account of how they're kin to you. The squatter's child from the island, turns out she's yours, Morgan J.'

He sat like stone. His palms wet and his eyes on stalks. As they passed into a tunnel his gaze was on the window and the last thing he saw was the fear in his face as his reflection died with the light.

———

Printed in Great Britain
by Amazon

42457991R00122